Forgotten Hearts

by
John Morgan

DEDICATION
To my wonderful Mum.
To those lost and those found.

'What the caterpillar perceives is the end is only the beginning for the butterfly.' I read this saying and knew it was the only way to begin describing the events that so profoundly changed me and so many others. But before you read this book, please know that I'm not a writer, yet this is a story I *must* tell, for my sanity and the debt of love I owe. If you allow it, this story will change you too.

ACKNOWLEDGMENTS
Caitrionia and Mary Waldron.

PART 1

Chapter 1

Sunday 18th September

'If this is old age, then you can keep it,' Walter said to Ted.

The dog, stiff from sleep and arthritis, shook himself and then scratched the door, his claws insistent against the wood. Walter lowered his paper. Ted wagged his tail.

Walter didn't really feel up to a walk – come to think of it, he had been more tired than usual recently – but Ted was whining softly and had placed his head on Walter's lap.

Walter smiled wearily. 'Nearly time, boy. Sure you're better than the old clock.' He took off his slippers and put his feet into his leather shoes. He tried to bend to reach his laces but stopped on the way down to put his hand on his back and purse his lips. Ted barked in sympathy.

'There's life in the old dog yet,' Walter said when he eventually managed to knot the laces.

He picked up the dog's lead and Ted gave a quick joyful yelp. 'Calm down, boy! Neither of us is pups anymore,' Walter chided him. What was wrong with Ted today? It was as if there was an urgent reason they should be sitting at *their* bench at the Botanic Centre.

Just as Walter set his trilby on his head and wrapped himself in his great coat, he realised he'd forgotten to take his bitter-tasting iron tonic, now a daily ritual for him. As he went back into the kitchen to get it, he could hear 'Pennies From Heaven' playing softly on the radio. He decided to leave it on so it would sound like someone was home.

Walter opened the locks on the door, each making a heavy click. Once the door was open, Ted strained to get out. Walter had just enough time to grab his blackthorn walking stick before he was tugged out the door.

They stepped out onto the suburban street and trundled along the row of sleeping red brick buildings. The houses, built for the new professionals of the 1930s, were now crumbling and the street was littered with frost-covered rubbish. It smelled of decay and cats. Walter longed for the shelter of his secluded bench at the gardens. He looked down at Ted, who watched him with bright mischief before tugging his lead again.

'Hold your horses, Ted!' Walter said, and started to wheeze. 'You'll be the death of me yet.'

The dog waited. Walter reached down to pat him and could feel, through the cold, wet roughness of Ted's fur, the warmth and softness of his skin beneath. If only Ted would let him put on the coat he had bought for him. But Ted was just as headstrong as his keeper and Walter was content that Ted would be fine until they reached the shelter of the Botanic Centre.

Once Walter had steadied himself, he shuffled on towards his bench at the Centre, the only place outdoors where an elderly person could sit without paying or freezing to death. It was more than that though: the huge steamy glass houses made him feel that he was holidaying in the sun. Walter had never owned a passport and relied on the television, on books and, most importantly, on his imagination to transport him to sunnier climes.

The day became a dull mist of rain and it was unseasonably cold; the splash of a red Sierra going past somehow made it feel even colder. Walter looked at the news headlines outside the local Mace shop: 'Elderly Couple Die Of Hypothermia After Gas Turned Off.'

What would happen to Ted if he wasn't here?

He hesitated and stroked the terrier's soggy fur. The dog raised his head, enjoying the kindness. 'Nearly there, boy. At my age, we're nearly there all the time. No, it won't be long, boy, for either of us.'

A teenager on a bicycle rode towards them on the narrow footpath. It was impossible to move out of the way without ending up on the road.

The teen stopped. 'Shift it!' he snarled.

Walter did what any gentleman would and politely ignored him. The boy rolled his eyes and swore under his breath. Suddenly, Ted shook his coat, spraying the teen with a fountain of water and contempt.

'Hey! I'll kill that mutt – and you, you old coffin dodger!' the boy yelled.

'Come on, Ted! We've got to go,' Walter said, swallowing both his anger and amusement.

The teen glared at them for a moment before making a rude hand gesture and cycling on, his bike's wheels skidding on the footpath. Walter patted Ted and noticed the mischievous look in the dog's eyes. Walter chuckled and patted him some more. Ted tugged on the lead again.

* * *

Margaret set the oak table with the gleaming knives and forks and rubbed her hands down her blue apron, standing back to admire her handiwork. She glanced at the clock and in an instant felt the panic tighten in her chest. She bit her lip and rushed back to the old rust-bitten oven while the warm smell of a cooking turkey filled the dilapidated house.

She pulled the glazed, golden bird out of the oven, her thin arms straining with the effort, and placed it on top of the cooker. She put a fork in and was relieved to see the juices running clear. Glancing at the antique kitchen clock, she was suddenly afraid to take her eyes off the bird.

As it cooled, she forced herself away from her vigil to run a duster over the pictures of her family. Her late husband's dark eyes glowered at her from inside the frame. He had been a dependable man in an undependable world, they said; a great oak that towered over this town's history. By contrast, their grandchildren, with the same small mouths, giggled and laughed in Spanish holiday snaps that stood beside Mr Brooks's formal portrait, while in another photograph, Margaret's daughter Rebecca sat proudly on her new jeep. The vehicle had cost Margaret most of her savings. 'Not that I begrudge her a penny,' Margaret murmured aloud.

As if trapped in the space between the past and her eternal duties to her family, her hand hovered over the silver frame of her husband's photograph. She had respected Mr Brooks – she still did. Mr Brooks (as he liked to be called, even by her) had chosen not only all her clothes – pale floral dresses – but also her lavender perfume. It had added to the feeling she'd had all her life that she didn't really exist – at least, not in the way proper human beings did.

While he had been alive he had forbidden her to come into his study, even to clean; even now the door to his study remained closed. He wasn't bad in any way – she had often heard him praised to the moon – and she had felt secure with his old-fashioned ways; 'standards have fallen, how times have changed,' he would say. He was dead ten years but she still missed his firm guidance. She still didn't know what to think or say without showing her naivety. Fortunately, she had Rebecca to guide her – the only person left to whom she could anchor her small world. Mr Brooks would have been proud of Rebecca, for she was firm like him. Margaret placed her hand on her heart and was about to sit down to count her blessings when she remembered. Heavens!

She blew a lock of frizzy hair from her eyes and returned to the kitchen just in time to stop the pot from boiling over. Heavens! There was a hiss of water.

Panic rose like bile into her throat as she heard voices outside the front door. Rebecca and the children had arrived. Margaret rushed to open the door even though Rebecca had a key. Her daughter had demanded one in case something happened to Margaret – in case she fell or … Margaret had thought a long time about it.

The grandchildren slouched sullenly through the door first. Michael and Martin, nine-year-old twins, were slightly overweight, tanned from their recent holiday and kitted out in matching fashionable clothes and trendy haircuts. They were quiet and probably bored, but Margaret knew this would soon transform into devilment.

'Hello Margaret,' Rebecca said as she came through the door.

Margaret nodded her head, her eyes downcast, her dutiful hands pressed against her dress.

The twins sat on her sofa, their muddy shoes leaving their customary trail. They quickly became engrossed in their PSPs, merely grunting at Margaret by way of a greeting. Margaret noted, not for the first time, that Rebecca's thick make-up and scanty leopard-print top would not have met with the approval of Mr Brooks.

Margaret thanked them for coming and quickly retreated to the kitchen as Rebecca inspected her mother's living room. Margaret peeped through the crack of the kitchen door and wondered if Rebecca would find the house up to standard, the nerves in her stomach eating away at her and spoiling her appetite.

She watched Rebecca gaze around the room, then run her hand over the photographs, her nimble fingers flicking away an invisible piece of dust. Then she looked at the antique clock, as she always did when she visited. 'I love that clock. Make sure it's me that gets it in the will,' Rebecca yelled. There really was no need to shout; her normal speaking voice could be heard in any room.

Margaret snatched the plates from a cupboard in the kitchen and slammed them down on the dining table that sat at one end of the living room. 'You're all I have. Who else am I going to leave it to?' was all she said. She fetched two plates of vegetables, steam rising, and set them on the grey mats on the oak table. The plates were her best; the turkey had cost more than her entire shopping bill for the previous week. If Rebecca and the kids showed only a moment's satisfaction with the meal it would be worth it.

'Yes, well.' Rebecca nodded, satisfied with Margaret's response. 'Boys, put down those games and come to the table! And try to remember – we've to be nice to Margaret.'

Margaret set a large plate of turkey down in front of Rebecca.

'I'm on a diet! How many times do I have to remind you, Margaret? How many times?'

Margaret lowered her eyes and hunched her shoulders as she returned to the kitchen. Eventually she came back with a small portion for herself, and after casting a quick look around to make sure everyone had everything they needed, she sat down. She closed her eyes in quiet prayer, thanking God for food and family. When she opened them again she found Rebecca looking contemptuously at her. Since Mr Brooks's death, their daughter had become scornful of religious faith.

Rebecca poured ketchup all over her meal and then added salt. She did the same for the twins.

'Maybe you should taste it first,' Margaret couldn't help saying. 'Just to see if you really need all that sauce – and salt is unhealthy.' As soon as she finished speaking, she put her hand over her mouth, trying to catch the words and force them back into her mouth.

'I know how I like your turkey and it's with plenty of sauce,' Rebecca barked back. 'Do you think I don't know my own children? And what the hell do you mean by unhealthy? Are you suggesting that I'm a bad mother?'

'I didn't mean any offence,' Margaret said, waving her hand in front of her as if to shoo the bad feeling away.

'I'm more of a mother than you've ever been,' Rebecca snapped. 'Anyway, I've been thinking what to do about you.' There was a long pause but she didn't go on.

'I don't want to go into a home,' Margaret said quietly.

'No, no, we wouldn't want you to do that. I've looked at the price of homes. You'd have to use my inheritance to pay for one!'

'Oh!'

'Something will have to be done though.' Rebecca screwed up her face. 'Why do you give me such large portions? It's very kind of you, but I need to watch my figure.' Nevertheless she continued to eat, her dinner disappearing in small mouthfuls.

Michael and Martin ate with their forks in one hand and their game consoles gripped in the other. The games beeped, trilled and made rude noises that unnerved Margaret.

'Yes. I'm the greatest monkey fighter of all time!' Martin yelled. He suddenly stood up on his chair.

Margaret's eyes widened. 'Oh, don't fall,' she shouted in her head.

'I can monkey you, Margaret,' Martin shouted.

Michael giggled and stood on his chair too. 'I'm the greatest monkey fighter of all time in the galaxy,' he pronounced.

'I'm the greatest in the universe,' said Martin.

'Don't be ruining Margaret's chairs,' Rebecca said giggling.

Margaret was more worried that the chairs wouldn't hold up to such treatment – they were antiques too. She pushed her own chair back from the table; it creaked and sighed as it slid over the worn carpet.

Then Michael jumped on to the table.

'Careful, you'll ...' Margaret began just as Michael knocked the dinner plate off the table. It smashed on the floor, splattering food and tomato sauce all over the carpet like blood at a crime scene. Everyone fell silent as Margaret, ashen-faced, stood up and rushed off for a cloth in the kitchen. She got to her knees and scrubbed at the carpet as the boys stood over her.

'Sorry!' Michael said, spluttering and giggling.

'That was a nice dinner – really ... tasty,' Rebecca said, trying not to laugh. 'Only you shouldn't use so much sage in the stuffing. Sorry about the kids. They're usually better behaved, but boys will be boys.'

The twins gathered up their games while Rebecca lifted her car keys off the table. She stared for a while at the old clock.

'I might take this in to be cleaned. You wouldn't mind?' Rebecca asked as she scooped the clock off the wall.

Margaret struggled to her feet. 'The clock? Well, if you think it's for the best. Only I've had it for a long time.'

At the front door, Rebecca pointed the key fob at the car to unlock it and the twins raced each other to it, pushing each other as they ran. A short time later they yelled from inside the car; one of them sounded the horn. Rebecca waved at them.

She turned and spoke to Margaret, the clock tucked under her arm: 'I suppose I'll see you next week.' She didn't try to disguise the resentment she felt at the burden Margaret had become.

Once they'd left, Margaret sat back in her favourite chair for a moment. It creaked with age, seeming to say 'Make do and mend'. It was her mantra. Then getting off the chair and onto her hands and knees, she began to scrub at the ketchup stain. But she already knew the carpet would never be clean.

* * *

Sundays were always difficult days for Rebecca. They were Margaret days. Why couldn't she just hurry up and die? Rebecca gasped at the harshness of the thought, yet it was becoming a persistent wish. She needed the money.

She wanted her husband back. She had dangled the prospect of acquiring her father's assets in front of Blake for a long time without it amounting to anything. Now, the economic downturn had ruined the desirability of property and, in turn, her desirability to her husband.

Rebecca gazed at her silent phone. She wished he would call. She checked that the volume was turned up, even though she had checked several times before. To distract herself she looked around the house with pride. Everything was almost as she wanted it. The house was clean and neat, the furniture modern and of the best design. Now she had an antique clock ready to sell. She needed a new television; her current one didn't have HD and the children needed an HD TV. And of course satellite was a must, and then the children needed Blu-ray – DVDs were so old hat.

One of the twins banged the DVD player with a biscuit, breaking her concentration. Her most prized possession, a colourful ceramic bird, wobbled precariously on the shelf above.

'Michael! Stop doing that – NOW!'

Michael's face flushed red. Eyes narrowed, he moved to the other side of the television and kicked the DVD player.

'Your father gave me that!' Rebecca shrieked as the ornamental bird rocked from side to side. She went towards him, but the shrill ring of her phone broke her train of thought. Michael banged the DVD with another biscuit in a rage at being scolded.

She reached for the phone. *Don't rush. Try to sound casual. It might not necessarily be Blake. It could be Margaret or any number of bores, and ... and ...* She picked up the phone.

'Hello?'

She held her breath and listened: 'Hi, this is Blue Horse Finance Payday Loans. May I speak to Rebecca Smith. You owe us —'

She slammed the phone down. The twins looked at her with bewilderment. The antique clock was suddenly ticking too loudly. She snatched up the phone and punched in her husband's phone number, prefixing it with 141 to disguise who was calling.

Martin joined Michael in bashing the DVD player with biscuits, wanting in on this new game that had attracted so much attention from their mother. But while their giggles filled the room, she had more important things on her mind.

'Hi, I just thought I'd call,' she eventually said into the receiver. She bit her lip. Oh God, she thought, I'm just as pathetic as a Margaret. 'I thought it might be a good time,' she went on. She clung onto the phone. 'Well, when can I call?'

His voice was clear and cool, sophisticated and callous: 'Darling, we've had this conversation before. It's over. I'm not interested in seeing you or those little brats again. It's time to move on. I don't want to make this into a joke.'

Nothing had changed, thought Rebecca. Yet like someone who keeps buying lottery tickets without winning anything, she refused to give up hope. She could hear someone talking in the background and knew it was his bit of fluff. Rebecca sank onto a low chair.

But within seconds she recovered and leapt to her feet. 'I know I said I wouldn't call, but I had to. It's about the kids. No, they're not sick. Listen …'

'Sorry, honey,' he cut in. 'You don't get to demand my attention any more. I married you and was kind enough to give your children a name. But you made me regret that kindness.'

'Sssshush, they'll hear! You're the only father they've known.'

Oblivious, he continued: 'And as for the money you owe me from the settlement, don't worry …'

Rebecca couldn't help sighing loudly with relief.

'Don't worry about the money,' he repeated. 'My solicitor will talk to yours.'

There was silence. This was always the moment when she choked on the memory of his cruelty. Countless times she had been with him when he held the phone away from his ear, rolling his eyes and sneering as the caller talked on. She never thought she would find herself on the receiving end.

Seconds lengthened to a minute as she waited for him to speak. Unable to bear it, she found herself doing what she always did – filled the silence with her own humiliation.

'It was ... it was my fault,' she said. 'I never should have thrown you out when I found out about her. I shouldn't have asked you to leave.'

The silence held. Was he there?

'You want me to beg?' she whined, collapsing into the chair once more. She wiped her eyes and pulled herself together. 'When are you taking the kids out? You're still their father ... Look it doesn't have to be like this ... I still love ... Hello? ... Don't hang up' – her voice tailed off – 'on me.'

She'd done it again, forced him to walk away. She stared at the phone keypad, contemplating calling him back.

Suddenly Martin kicked the DVD player so hard the little bird fell and smashed on top of it. The twins stared at the pieces that had burst onto the shag pile carpet and said nothing.

'I'm meant to have nothing. Nothing ... nothing ... nothing,' she howled at no one in particular.

She began to gather up the pieces, the sharp edges cutting into her hand making her bleed. Still, she could not stop holding them. 'Nothing,' she repeated as tears streamed down her cheeks and her shoulders heaved.

The antique clock chimed midnight.

Chapter 2

The sun hung low in the autumn sky. Walter twisted Ted's lead around his gnarled fingers, barely able to hold on to it as he bent over the grave. He lifted away last week's dying flowers and laid a fresh bunch on the grave, blessing himself as he did so.

With a J-cloth he cleaned the frosted green mildew off the headstone. It dated back ninety years; his own mother was the last person to be interred in this grave. She had passed away twenty years ago and the plot was almost full. He was the last of his line, so when he joined the others, the grave would be complete for eternity.

The gravestone, carefully inscribed each year it welcomed a new occupant, marked the graves of seven children – his brothers and sisters – and his mother. She had been the longest living relative in his family, and if he lived another year he would overtake her for that title. That was something he often thought about these days – dying.

His mother had had such a hard time. Each of her children had died in infancy. She had tried to hold on to them but they were born sickly and weak and no amount of nurture could save them. The doctor had recommended – for her health and her husband's sanity – that she should have no more. Yet she clung onto the hope that became Walter. His father's mission on earth complete, he died of a heart attack shortly after Walter's birth.

Walter was taught the names of his brothers and sisters as if they were a childhood rhyme: Isaac, Harold, Albert, Maggie, Annie, Kathleen and Sarah. Walter's mother often reminded him of each of them and told him that for their sake he had to make her proud. She had held tightly onto him. The song 'A Mother's Love's A Blessing' began playing in his head and he sang aloud 'Keep her while she's living, You'll miss her when she's gone.' His singing, though tuneless and feeble, was heartfelt and sincere.

Ted whined.

'I'll be done in a minute, boy,' Walter reassured him. 'It just takes a little longer to show care and attention when you're old.'

He squinted at the grave. It might have been better if he'd joined them sooner rather than later. Sometimes he appreciated the beauty of the world and found solace in Ted's companionship, but lately he'd noticed the harshness of the winters and, too often, wondered what he had achieved, what the point of it all was.

Ted pawed his leg. 'Right! I'm done now, Ted,' he said.

He had dedicated his life to caring for his mother when she was alive and now he dedicated himself to tending the family's grave. He tipped his hat down and shuffled back through the cemetery. A car slowly drove past. Ted barked at the wheels. Cars should never be allowed in here, Walter thought. Cemeteries aren't places for cars; it was wrong.

Walter often let Ted off the lead. In his younger years, he'd run off and all Walter could hear was his distant barking. Now Ted always stayed at his side, even when he was off his lead, though Walter worried that he would forget his doggy years to dart off after a stray cat.

* * *

As Walter entered the Botanic Centre gardens he could feel the temperature rise. The place seemed to have a weather system all of its own. He walked to their sheltered outdoor bench; mild air blew over from the garden. He scanned the empty path and iron benches. Only those who needed to escape their houses would come on a day like this. Who was interested in botany in these days of newfangled television and cheap flights to faraway places?

Like a pair of bookends, Ted sat at one end of the bench while Walter sat at the other reading the *Guardian*. He was methodical with the newspaper; he would read every word and then wedge it in the bench for someone else to read.

Ted was alert, his head tilting to one side and then to the other. Suddenly, he jumped off the bench and, with his leather lead trailing behind him, walked off. Walter dropped his paper as Ted made his way down to the main path and disappeared round the corner.

'Ted! Ted!' called Walter forgetting his age and dashing after him.

He arrived just in time to see Ted jump up at a lady coming up the path. For a moment the lady looked horrified, then her face flushed with pleasure and surprise.

Walter ran up and grabbed Ted's lead. 'Please accept my apologies,' he said. 'This is the first time he's ever done this. Are you all right?'

The woman said nothing – just stared at him.

Walter began to panic. He touched his chest and rubbed his arm. 'Please sit down a moment. There's a bench just over here.'

The lady didn't respond. Instead she looked down at her shoes and smiled.

'Well, as long as you're okay?' Walter said, tipping his trilby at her. Ted wagged his tail and sat down in front of her as if waiting for her decision.

The lady was wearing a coat that had seen better days and old-fashioned shoes. She looked down shyly at her feet and eventually nodded.

'What a wonderful dog,' she said as they began the walk to Walter's bench. 'I can't believe he's so ... *friendly*.'

Ted barked as if to say thank you.

When they sat down on the bench Ted barked again and pawed the lady's knee. She tenderly stroked his fur and Ted licked her hand.

Walter cleared his throat. 'My name, madam, is Walter and it's a great pleasure to meet you.'

'My name is Margaret,' replied the lady, blushing. 'And it's an equal pleasure to meet you and your dog. What's his name?'

'Ted.'

Ted woofed as Margaret shook Walter's hand.

'I haven't seen you here before. I would've noticed,' Walter said.

'How would you have noticed me?'

It was Walter's turn to blush. 'I come here every day. It gives the dog a chance to stretch his legs and saves on the heating bills. I love the smell of the plants and I get to see people even if they don't speak to me.'

'He's beautiful that dog. What kind of dog is he?'

'A Yorkshire terrier. He thinks he's still a pup the way he gets on. You wouldn't guess his age.'

'I wouldn't try,' said Margaret, smiling.

'He's fourteen years old. In doggie years that makes him even older than my seventy-five winters.'

'I wouldn't have thought you were seventy-five!'

Walter was unexpectedly pleased by her remark but only raised his eyebrows.

Just then, Margaret stood up and began to shuffle away, her shoes barely making a noise on the paving. 'I get things wrong all the time,' she said apologetically. 'If I didn't have my Rebecca to help me, I don't know what would become of me. I'd better go.'

Walter winced and got up too. 'No, I'm sorry. Thanks for the compliment – I'm not used to them. Me and my dog walk here all the time and no one notices that we even exist – except for kids, who stare at me and Ted as if they're wondering if mugging us is worth the effort.'

Margaret laughed and turning towards Walter said, 'I'm not sure anyone would want to mug your wee doggie. He doesn't have much to take.'

'I'm pretty safe too,' said Walter. 'I've got the pensioner's best protection – poverty. I've nothing worth stealing.'

Margaret laughed again.

Walter liked the sound of her laugh. Then she suddenly became self-conscious again. Her pale wrinkled skin flushed red. Ted barked and pulled on the lead.

'Do you live far away?' Walter asked. The rain began again, making a determined noise on the thick glass and Perspex roof.

Margaret didn't answer.

An uncertain Walter tipped his hat.

Margaret nodded and then disappeared down the path.

Walter turned to begin his own drab journey home, but he changed his mind and set off along a different route home, a route he hadn't taken since he was a lad. Everything looked vibrant and shiny and new in the rain.

Chapter 3

Sunday 2nd October

It was a week since she had met Walter and Ted, and Margaret had found herself thinking about them often. It was a bright spot in her otherwise dull life.

'Oh! The turkey …'

She rushed into the kitchen to check the turkey. It was cooked; she was sure. Well, mostly sure. She checked it again for the umpteenth time. Done. Now she just had to wait for Rebecca's call that they were on their way. She inadvertently glanced over at the space where the clock used to be and hung her head.

She had inherited the clock from her mother and it was one of the few things that she had left of her. At least if Rebecca has it it would be still in the family, she thought. Margaret had never known her own mother; she had died in childbirth. So she had been brought up to be a proper lady, with no ambitions beyond getting married and being a housewife. She had been lucky to escape working in the mill, but she still felt as if she had had little success in life. Rebecca was precious to her, but what else had she to show for it? Her role as a wife was over, and she had failed as a mother and granny. Rebecca didn't need her, and she certainly never wanted to be a burden. But with the shops so far away and the lack of buses, Margaret had to rely on Rebecca even more. Margaret knew that was why Rebecca had been confident her mother would give her the money for the jeep if she asked.

Margaret returned to the living room, sat in her rocking chair and twisted the wedding band that had been on her finger these past fifty years. Sometimes the ring left a green stain around her finger. As she rocked in the chair, she pictured in her head a woman in a foreign land moving backwards and forwards in prayer to her departed Messiah. Margaret glanced over at her clock again. It was still gone. Her time had been taken ... stolen ... borrowed. Borrowed, never to be returned.

Where on earth was Rebecca? She'd been careful not to use so much sage this time. Margaret stopped rocking and since the phone was beside her, she picked it up and listened to the dialling tone. If it had a broken tone it meant there was a message. Rebecca had taught her to press 1571 to get her messages, so she pressed 1571 anyway: 'You have no messages.' Then Margaret pressed 1471: 'You were called on the twenty-fifth of September.' No one had called since last week. She started to dial Rebecca's number, then stopped. What if Rebecca was busy? Or perhaps one of the children was sick? She put down the receiver. She would try to keep the food warm and not call. But what if she'd had an accident? Were they okay?

Margaret snatched up the phone and called Rebecca's mobile number, closing her reddened, watery eyes tightly while she waited for Rebecca to answer.

'What?' Blunt and to the point. Typical Rebecca.

'Rebecca, are you ... okay?'

'Am I okay? Are you okay?'

'Yes.' Margaret made herself small in the chair.

'Then why are you calling?'

'I was wondering if you and the twins are coming for dinner today.'

'Do you not think if we were coming we'd be there by now?'

'Yes. That's why I'm phoning ...'

'Do I have to explain my every movement to you? I thought the kids might enjoy a day out at the park. They're having a lovely time playing here. *Fresh air.*'

'Sorry. I'll not bother you then. But I'll put some turkey in the fridge, so if you feel like some later, it'll be here for you.'

'Have you not been listening, Margaret? I think you need checked for dementia.'

'Bye. Sorry. Bye ... Bye.'

* * *

Michael and Martin were sitting on a bench playing their hand held gamers.

'Monkey fighter!' said Martin. 'Double
monkey fighter!' said Michael.

Rebecca surveyed the park where children had played football and stick-in-the-mud in all weathers for years, but which was now a wasteland for drunks and the homeless and God knows what other kind of people. She quailed at the thought of her home being repossessed and needed a drink. A tramp came into view and it began to rain.

'Pull up your hoods in the rain. Come on, time for home,' she said to the kids. 'While we still have one,' she murmured quietly to herself. 'While. We. Still. Have. One.'

* * *

As Sunday afternoon dragged by without any visitors, Margaret sat back on her rocking chair trying to summon the energy that Rebecca had sapped. Rebecca was overbearing, but she had to be tough – bringing up two children as a single mum was difficult. Margaret should be thinking of more ways to help.

She chided herself, recalling another of Mr Brooks's sayings – 'Laziness, did I ever offend thee?' – and putting her feet into her brown slippers, shuffled back into the kitchen. She sliced the turkey, put generous helpings on three willow-patterned plates and placed them in the fridge. She put a small amount on her own plate for her dinner. Margaret's appetite had dwindled recently and she'd lost weight, much to Rebecca's chagrin. Margaret had thanked her for her concern.

When she'd finished her dinner, without thinking about it or knowing why, she got ready to go out. As she pulled the front door behind her, pushing it three times to make sure it was secure, she recalled Walter's words, 'I've nothing worth stealing.' Shocked at herself, she quickly put her hand over her mouth.

* * *

The trees glistened and the grass was wet underfoot. Her old shoes were letting in water as she splashed through puddles. Normally, this would be enough to make her turn back, but today she *had* to go on.

She walked past the garage with its 'For Sale' sign. The recession was as tough as anyone remembered, with pensioners and the poor catching the worst of it. Mr Brooks used to condemn layabouts and the single mothers who produced them over his coffee and *Daily Mail*. Yet the off-licences and bookies still thrived, and open now on Sundays. How was she any different to those layabouts?

She wondered why she was walking to the Botanic Centre. It would take her past the playground; if Rebecca saw her, she might think she'd come to drag her home for her dinner, like one of those wives that fetches their wayward husband home from the pub. Margaret hoped the rain would have made Rebecca retreat to the car. She didn't walk this way often, for the park was used by teenagers mad with drink and drugs. She hoped the cold would keep them away too.

As she turned the corner, she was struck by the beauty of the glass building. The Botanic Centre looked like a fairy castle. *What a childish thought!*

* * *

At the door to the Centre was a sign which said, 'No dogs except guide dogs'. It was strange that she'd never noticed it before. Hidden in the vegetation was a carving of a wooden angel plucking the strings of a sitar. This was so unusual – she struggled for the word to describe it – startling. Without her glasses she strained to make out the plaque. It read: 'Hindu Goddess Saraswati'. Another wooden statue – a child, smiling stoically, with its knees pressed against its chest – was nearby.

She loosened her clothing as the penetrating dampness retreated. The metal grills underfoot rattled with each step she took and it sounded ominous to Margaret. She felt sure something good would happen; even if didn't at least she'd got out of the house.

And then she spotted him; even with her poor eyesight she knew it was the lovely man with his nice dog.

* * *

Walter raised his hat and Margaret lowered her eyes. Having no scruples, Ted barked and jumped up at her. She gasped and then gave them a beautiful smile – or so thought Walter. Ted wagged its tail and Margaret glowed.

Walter, dressed in his best suit that he usually reserved for funerals, stood up and politely greeted her by tipping his trilby. He bent down and stroked Ted's head. 'I just don't know what gets into this dog sometimes? He doesn't do that with anyone else. Would you be so kind as to join us, Madam?' he asked with a bow.

Ted looked at Margaret expectantly, ears forward and eyes wide, a front paw hovering in mid air.

Margaret made her way towards the air-conditioned bench and sat down stiffly. Walter sat down too, leaving a respectable distance between them on the bench.

'I hope you don't mind me asking you to join us,' Walter said.

'No, not at all. It's just that I'm not used to people, to talking … to mixing … outside.' Margaret stared straight ahead into the distance.

'Outside?'

'Outside my home. I don't usually talk to strangers in places other than my home. Or even in my home, to be honest.'

'I lead a quiet life too.'

Ted lay at Margaret's feet and wagged his tail, brushing off some of the dirt on her shoes that had accumulated on her journey there.

'You're the first person to take an interest in Ted,' Walter said. 'He's my family.'

Margaret smiled. Walter liked her warm and unassuming smile. It reassured him and she clearly had a connection with Ted.

She leaned forward and patted the dog's head. He pulled his ears back, welcoming the affection. That was another thing Ted had never done with anyone other than Walter.

Suddenly, Margaret began gently weeping. Walter handed her a pristine cloth handkerchief that he kept in his pocket. His mother had always advised that a gentleman should carry a handkerchief. It was the first time he'd had occasion to use it.

Margaret blew her nose. There was a long pause. 'My daughter and grandchildren visit me occasionally. I count my blessings. They are my life, as it should be, and ... I never wanted to be a burden to them.'

Walter licked his lips nervously. He said the only thing he could think of. 'Would you like some tea? I usually go to Helen's, but sometimes the day before my pension comes I bring a flask.'

Margaret glanced at her shoes before she finally asked, 'What about your wife?'

'I never married.' Walter had always dreaded the issue of his bachelor status; it had been considered a suspicious character flaw by his colleagues. Indeed, it had always been a issue until he was turned forty – 'Why did you not ...?' 'Was there ever ...?' Even 'You're not, are you?' He was old-fashioned enough to believe that some things were private. It had just never happened for him, and it never happened for a good reason. Walter picked an invisible piece of lint from his suit jacket, hoping the topic would change.

'I can hardly remember a time before my marriage,' said Margaret.

Walter blushed.

As Margaret raised her head and stared into space, Walter pulled a flask out of the bag at his feet. He offered her a cup. It was the only cup he had but he didn't want Margaret to know that. He unscrewed the lid of the flask and poured steaming tea with the milk already in it into the cup that she held.

'Do you take sugar?' he asked. Sugar was his own guilty pleasure.

For a moment Margaret looked as if she was expecting someone else to answer. Then with a shake of her head she said, 'No, Rebecca told me that sugar isn't good for me.' There was a long pause before she added, 'Though she does take two sugars herself.'

Walter reached back into his bag and pulled out a bone for Ted, who began to gnaw on it contentedly at their feet.

Margaret pointed to a flower. 'What's it called?' she asked.

'Do you like it?'

Taken aback, she blinked. 'I'm not sure.'

Walter wondered why she didn't seem to have opinions or perhaps it was just that she was afraid to express them. She did seem to be curious about things. Walter had been interested in the flower too and had looked it up in the library. It was outwardly unattractive, but inside, something special happened.

'It seems to have been here as long as I can remember, though most people don't notice it.' Walter tugged his ear uncertainly. 'It's an agave plant – a century plant. It blooms once and then dies. I used to think it only bloomed once a century, but it flowers every thirty years.'

Margaret clasped her hands together. 'If it never knew life it wouldn't mind dying.'

Walter drew back, shocked at the unexpected depth of her response. 'Everything dies eventually. The person who named it felt like that too. He nicknamed it a "corpse plant". But I guess what you never know you never miss – at least, that's what Cat Stevens said so it must be true. What happens are small sprouts at the plant's base carry on the long growing cycle. I guess that old age can be a time for new beginnings. Winston Churchill's career seemed over in 1932, but then in 1942, at the age of sixty-six, he became Prime Minister. And then there was that other person who bought a small burger restaurant when he was fifty-five that became McDonalds. ... But I'm speaking when I should be listening!'

Ted took a break from chewing to look up at them.

Margaret half stood. 'Oh, I'm sorry. Did I insult you?'

'How insult?' asked Walter, scratching his head. 'Did I argue?' She set the cup down.

'No! Expressing an opinion is not …' Walter watched as confusion sparked in her eyes. He sighed as Margaret sat down again, though she continued to stare into space. Walter leaned over and placed his hand on Ted's head, stroking him for reassurance. Margaret lifted the cup again and sipped the tea tentatively.

'Is it okay?' Walter asked, 'Not too strong or too weak or ...' 'Do you know that this is the first cup of tea I've had that I haven't made myself.'

'What?'

'Really. At least, as far as I can remember. … Oh, there was one time, long ago, when my father took me to a tea shop to meet Mr Alfred Brooks. We only met the once before he married me. What was the tea shop called? I still recall what it looked like. … It was called the Copper Spoon.' Margaret nodded emphatically.

'Why, I remember that shop too! It's thirty years since it closed. You must be a very private person,' Walter said, wondering what kind of life this woman had led.

'I … I'm not.' Margaret frowned. She looked like she was trying hard to find the right words.

'You're not private?' Walter ventured.

'I'm not a person,' Margaret said quietly.

Walter gasped, but refrained from speaking. Instead he scrutinised her closely, observing her dowdy clothes, the way she never met his eyes, the way she walked with her head down watching the ground. She seemed almost listless, as if the life had been sucked out of her and when she wasn't smiling she looked older than he guessed she probably was. Yet he sensed a soul locked in there somewhere. During his working life, he'd been good at detecting depth of character. And then, of course, there was Ted's judgment, which he trusted implicitly. Walter knew he needed to choose his words carefully, but what could he say?

'Margaret …'

Suddenly Margaret returned the cup; the tea had gone. 'I've just realised that I make a terrible cup of cha!' she announced.

Walter laughed at her ready wit and the awkwardness of this situation. He glanced at Ted, who seemed to be smiling too.

She blushed at his laughter; then panic immediately flitted across her eyes. Walter wondered about this. 'You're laughing at me,' she said.

'Not in a cruel way. Why would I do that to such an interesting and warm ... lady? Look! Even Ted's laughing at your joke,' he said, smiling.

'Dogs can laugh?'

'Yes! Look carefully at his mouth. You see the way it curls up slightly – and look at the mischievousness in his eyes. He's enjoying your company too!'

'Too?'

'I think we need a proper cup of tea, and Ted could use a sausage. Isn't that right, boy?'

Ted barked knowingly. Ted knew he had made a friend and Walter dared hope that he had made one too.

* * *

It was another slow Sunday afternoon, and Helen was singing 'You are my sunshine' as she lovingly wiped down the tables in her café. She was wearing a white apron, spotless despite the fries she constantly cooked, and her cheeks glowed, adding to the matronly appearance that her customers found so comforting.

Truth be told, most afternoons were slow now. Her pride was the only thing that kept her from closing, like the rest of the shops on the terrace, but she knew she'd never recapture the success of the 1980s, when construction workers filled the place. She wondered sometimes if she held onto the past too tightly. Her way of life was dying through no fault of her own. Helen was an expert in sausage rolls, fries and people, and refused to allow melancholy thoughts to arrest her cheerfulness, another thing her customers liked about her.

The temperature inside rose, steaming the windows up. She thought about her heating bill and her other overheads. The government was always talking about making things cheaper but never seemed to. Her café was clean but a little shabby – she just didn't have the money to refurbish. Now it was all rules and regulations – certain things at certain temperatures and hygiene scores that had to be put in notes in the doors. She was just thankful that she'd got four stars so far. Every moment she worried was a moment she wouldn't get back, and whenever she felt the recession bite she just put took a deep breath and put on a big smile.

She didn't even like the name of the café – Helen's Kitchen. It wasn't named by or for her; it bore the name of the original proprietor, her mother Helen McDonald, and out of respect it had remained unchanged. It could have been worse – it could have been called McDonald's, her surname, instead!The café stank of fries – the junk food of her generation – mixed with the pungent smell of tea, coffee, and Dettol. The air freshener she sprayed the place with every evening only seemed to exacerbate the strange lingering odour and made its own contribution to the ambience. She hoped she would never get completely used to the smell. It was the smell of safety, the scent of a different era cocooned in a modern town, a quiet oasis in the midst of a busy world. Smiling, she wiped her clean hands on her apron and continued humming her cheerful song. To hell with poverty, she thought.

One of her regulars, Joe, sat reading *The Sun* and munching a fry-up at a table towards the front of the café. Helen glanced at him as she cleaned. He was quite an attractive, rugged man with dark hair, a stereotypical workman, as if God had been giving him guidance in the career he should choose. He came every Sunday and stayed so long that Helen often wondered if he had a home to go to. He was a good customer, though not a good tipper.

Helen walked over to the window at the front of the café and gave it a good wipe. She glanced at the empty street outside: there was litter all over the place – the detritus of modern Britain. She tried to make sure her own doorstep was always clean and regularly had to brush up empty bottles of Buckfast, fast-food packaging, cigarette butts, whatever had been left by the Saturday night winos.

Joe the workman yawned, stretched and looked at his watch. Then he wiped his chin clean of egg and belched. Helen, standing with her back to him, rolled her eyes. Suddenly she spied two customers coming towards her café. It was another regular, Walter, with his little dog, and Walter had someone with him – a lady friend. The bell tinkled above the door to announce their arrival

'Walter!' Helen greeted him enthusiastically. 'This is the first time you've brought your missus. You're a dark horse, you are. I thought it was just you and wee Ted!' She walked round behind the counter.

Walter blushed; Margaret blanched.

Helen beamed at them and waved her chubby hands in the air excitedly. 'I'll make you both a nice hot cup of tea, and I'm sure I can find a sausage for Ted.' Ted cocked his head to one side and eyed Helen expectantly. 'Take a seat!'

Walter and Margaret made their way over to a table and sat down opposite each other. Ted sat beside Margaret and patiently waited. Margaret stared at the table top and refused to make eye contact with either Walter or Helen.

'Oh dear, Mrs Walter, you don't look too well,' said Helen. 'I'll put some sugar in your tea.'

'I'm afraid you've got the wrong idea, Helen. This lady and I are just acquaintances,' Walter explained, taking his trilby off and setting it on the table. He dared not use the word 'friend'.

'Mother of God, you can't fool me! I've run this café since my mother died nigh on twenty-five years ago and you make a beautiful couple.'

Joe burped as he walked to the counter to pay.

'I'll be with you in a moment. These two customers are in dire need of a cuppa,' Helen said to him over her shoulder. She filled two mugs with steaming hot tea from a large pot brewing on the cooker and brought them over to the table.

'There ya go, lovebirds.'

It was as if Margaret snapped out of a daze. 'What am I doing here?' she asked all flustered. 'My Rebecca might call the house. She'll think I've abandoned them. And Mr Brooks's anniversary is next week. How can I … Oh my! I'm going to have to go.' And with that she took out her purse and stood up.

'Any chance of you taking for mine, love?' Joe asked, picking his ear with a fiver.

But Helen was too engrossed with Walter and his friend and suddenly realised the extent of their discomfort.

Walter stood up too. 'No, Madam. Please, finish your tea first ... or at least let me pay ...'

'I pay my own way!' Margaret said firmly as she shuffled towards the counter.

Walter opened his battered brown leather wallet and followed her. 'Let me at least pay for my own.'

Margaret hesitated for a moment and then nodded. She took out an old purse with a clasp fastening and plucked out a pound coin, which she set on the counter. Walter set his own pound down beside it. Helen smiled as cheerfully as she could as she slid the coins off the counter.

'Let me walk you home,' Walter said, following Margaret to the door.

'Really sorry. I'm really sorry,' muttered Margaret. With a jingle the door opened and she walked out into the biting northern breeze.

'What's wrong with your friend?' Helen asked. 'Was the tea okay?'

Walter shrugged, and he and Ted left the café as quickly as they could.

Helen caught Joe's eye and took the fiver from him; it was the exact amount.

'The service is great in this café – when you can get it,' Joe said pleasantly.

Helen made a play of scuffing his ear and he smiled. She watched the old man hurry off down the street after his friend. She hoped they would come again. She made a mental note to be on her best behaviour next time.

Chapter 4

Sunday 9th October

Walter sat in his armchair beside the open fire. The fireplace had seen better days and he often found it hard to light a decent fire without a lot of sputtering . Why was it so difficult? A bit like himself, eh? But he was better off than most people – it wasn't yet a case of choosing between heat or food for him.

It had been exactly a week since he had seen Margaret; he had thought about her often since then. During the previous week he had found himself lingering in the Botanic Centre longer than normal. He stared at the clock on the stone mantelpiece. She was an unusual woman, but he liked her, though he was not sure if she liked him. He checked his watch. Feeling restless, Walter struggled up out of the chair and took his mother's wedding ring off the fireplace. He rolled it between his fingers; the circle meant no beginning and no end – forever. His mother had specifically made him promise he would treasure it forever. *Forever.*

His mother had instilled in him a respect for women and it made him a little shy with them. Mother had always known what to say and do, and he knew that she probably would not have understood the sense of loneliness that had dogged him all his life. Nor would she have appreciated his current thoughts about Margaret. But she would have found fault in some way. He didn't quite know how to resolve this.

Mother had told him that his head should always rule his heart and that was advice he had lived by. But up until recently, his head and his heart had agreed and Mother didn't need to tell him what to do. Then Margaret came along and seemed to fulfil a need he didn't even know he had. It was the most powerful feeling he'd ever experienced. He didn't understand it at all.

He knew that Ted was asleep in his bed upstairs; he tended to do that when the central heating was on.

'Ted! We're going for a walk,' Walter called. 'Ted, where's your lead?'

Seconds later, the dog came slowly down the stairs, his eyes blinking in the light, his routine upset.

'Surprised myself too, doggie.'

* * *

Walter and Ted trundled along through the gloom of the leafless trees and the soggy undergrowth, a solitary car swishing along the wet road beside them. They made their way to the Botanic Centre, not stopping to look at Mother's grave; Walter decided he would do that later. The footpath was slippery and hazardous, but the journey was too important to delay. He had waited sixty years already. Eventually, he reach their bench.

Although he knew that the café's welcoming doors would be open at that time, he somehow felt more at ease sitting on his bench among the other living things.

Sunday was here and so were they.

* * *

Rebecca, clutching the phone, prepared her opening line: 'I know it's a Sunday …'

She caught a glimpse of her herself in the mirror as she picked up the phone. She stood sideways and sucked her stomach in, smoothing the fabric of her top over her hips. Her husband – soon-to-be ex-husband – Blake used to compliment her on her figure, although after a few years of marriage he had kept adding 'for your age'. She had taken to pounding on a running machine, as if trying to reverse time. No matter what she did, it never seemed to satisfy him. Once, he had referred to her body as a piece of gristle! If hadn't been for her darling boys …

'I know it's a Sunday …,' she repeated.

She dropped the phone and went for a shower. The twins carried on watching television, oblivious to their mother's desperation.

As she stood under the scalding jet of water, she spat the words out, water spraying over the shower curtain and running down it like sweat. 'I know it's a Sunday ...' She lingered there, lost in thought and enjoying the prickling sensation of hot water on her skin. But she couldn't stay lost for too long; she needed to make that call and the water would grow cold soon.

She dressed quickly and carefully, slipping into a leopard-print dress that made her feel like a predator again. Blake and his friends had nicknamed her 'Cougar', which she knew was no compliment. Rebecca had always wanted to give the impression that she was fierce in love and business. Yet the ageing process had taken the edge off that fierceness; Blake had devoured her best years and then cast her off, leaving her with no idea of who or what she was.

Why would Blake want to talk to her? There was nothing more he wanted from her – he had already taken everything he could. The only thing left was the kids – he could try to take sole custody of them, claim she was an unfit mother who liked too much Sauvignon Blanc. Rebecca smiled wryly; he didn't want the children any more than he wanted her. But she shared the kids with him and he knew how much they meant to her; he might decide to pursue them just to spite her.

She had borrowed, scraped together, begged and paid him every penny she could. He somehow knew about all her secret bank accounts, even the one in the Icelandic Bank that she'd set up for the twins. He knew her 'exact worth', he said, and he meant more than her monetary worth.

'I know it's a Sunday,' she repeated. She picked up the receiver. His number was etched in her memory. Taking a large gulp of air, she called him at his penthouse.

'What?'

'I know it's Sunday but I need a few more days to—'

Blake snorted. 'For God's sake, give me peace! Like I said, my solicitor will talk to yours. We ran out of conversation about two years ago.'

'I've no way of paying you,' said Rebecca, biting her bottom lip, doing her best to stop herself from saying what she always said. And before she could stop herself, out it popped again: 'Come back. I need you. The kids need … Hello? … Hello? … Hello?'

Rebecca was about to redial when the phone buzzed. She hit the reply button straight away. 'We must have got cut off ...'

'It's just me, Rebecca.'

'Margaret! What the hell do you want?'

'Can you come ... over please?'

'No I cannot! Do you think you can just summon me and I'll appear?' Tears dripped down her cheeks and onto the phone, salting her words and stinging her lips.

'I was hoping we could have a chat,' said Margaret.

'You're nothing but a burden.'

'I'm sorry.'

'You're always sorry. I'll come when I can, okay?'

'Fine. Thank you, my dear.'

Rebecca hung up and threw the phone against the wall. The twins came in to investigate. She stood with her back to them and cried, her face hidden behind her hands.

'Mummy! … Mummy!' they shouted in unison. 'What did the phone do to you?' They burst into a fit of giggles at their wit.

She needed a drink.

* * *

Blake drank his aged whiskey neat from a crystal glass. He was a connoisseur in many things. From where he sat he could see the beautiful seventeen-year-old, Louise, lying in his bed, the red walls of his bedroom giving the impression of a bordello. He worked out; he looked after himself; sex was important to him; it confirmed that he was powerful. He locked the drinks cabinet with a click and went to his study. Finishing the whiskey in a single gulp he set the glass on his desk for Louise to collect and wash.

Putting on white cotton gloves he took out his first edition Nietzsche. He liked to handle it, to look at the German writing, to feel the thickness of the pages and the way they turned. This was his bible. He admired Nietzsche's theories of Man and Superman, of master–slave morality; he believed himself to be exceptional – a true master.

Blake was not evil; he would not harm anyone for the sake of it. He was a realist. People were driven by hunger, sexual appetite, money and vanity; they were slaves to these desires. Others – intellectuals, superior people – must bear the burden of being masters.

Rebecca was no longer a necessity in his life. He knew why she needed him. She'd never had the pain of making choices when she was with him. Now she had grown older, more desperate, clingy. He replaced the book in the cupboard and decided to return to Louise. He took off the gloves; he didn't need to handle her with the same care.

Back in the bedroom, he slipped under the black sheets and looked at his own reflection in the mirror suspended from the ceiling over the bed. Louise put her arm around him. He didn't much like emotional intimacy and had learned to fake it to get what he wanted, but once his needs were met he found any kind of closeness irritating. He tolerated Louise's arm for a few moments, then brushed it off and got out of bed again.

He strolled to the bathroom and splashed on a little aftershave – Obsession it was called; Rebecca had bought it for him. Suddenly he noticed something in the mirror that sent a chill through him: the beginnings of a bald spot. It seemed that even he wasn't immune to ageing.

* * *

Margaret stifled a cry as she picked up the phone receiver and checked again to see if Rebecca had called. She really wished she would. She was so lucky she had Rebecca in her life. Without Rebecca ... well, it didn't bear thinking about. She'd have no one, no one at all.

Losing Mr Brooks had made her feel rudderless, frightened and impoverished. She had used a large portion of her savings for his funeral – Mr Brooks had no life insurance policy, or if he did, she hadn't been able find it. Rebecca had taken what was left of her savings and Margaret had survived ever since on her basic state pension. She had had to make do and mend. Rebecca had told her that her financial problems were down to her own mismanagement – the house was too warm; she should take showers, not baths (she didn't have a shower in the house). Rebecca thought Margaret had too much of a lot of things and insisted on helping her get rid of any excess.

Margaret put the phone back in the charger. It hadn't rung in a week, but she needed to keep the phone fully charged just in case Rebecca called. She looked at Mr Brooks's desk sitting at the far side of the study. It was still locked even though it had been ten years since he passed. It was sturdy, like the man himself. She knew from the antiques valuer that Rebecca brought along one day that the desk had a secret drawer. The valuer had looked around the house disparagingly until he saw the desk and had brightened as some men do when talking about money. He had told her about the drawer. Margaret sometimes wondered if it contained valuables or the missing insurance policy, but Rebecca had forbidden her to open it. The desk was worth more than everything combined that Rebecca had taken for 'restoration', 'repair' or 'cleaning'. Surely Rebecca wouldn't dare to take it too. Would she?

Margaret began dusting. She looked at Mr Brooks's photograph, his eyes seeming to follow her around the room. 'I tried to please you and everybody else,' she said to him. But in the end she'd pleased no one. She became breathless and sat on a rickety chair rather than Mr Brooks's rich red leather chair. She swallowed hard and sighed deeply, exhausted by her exertions and her thoughts.

She could no longer walk to church; it was too far and Rebecca couldn't afford the time or the diesel to take her. She couldn't even kneel down because of her bad knees, but she always made sure to drop her head when she turned towards the wooden cross on the wall beside her husband's desk.

Margaret's prayers were to Saint Theresa who had never failed in intercession. She prayed for Mr Brooks, he might pray for her; for her daughter, that the Lord might help her find peace; for the twins, that they might grow up safe and happy. Lately she had said prayers for Walter and Ted, that they would not become disappointed in their new friend too soon. The Lord looked down on her from his cross but gave no sign.

Maybe she could get to church at the weekend – sit at the back, donate what little money she had. But the buses only ran every two hours, so it would be hard to get home again. She couldn't afford a taxi and make a donation – it was one or the other – and she knew that even a miracle wouldn't encourage Rebecca to darken the church door.

At Mr Brooks's funeral the priest had promised that he would visit Margaret as 'often as he could', but he was busy with other parishioners who seemed to need him more. She was grateful that he still included her in the church roof fundraising circular that arrived in the post every Monday – she glanced over at one lying out in the hallway. They were still addressed to Mr Brooks.

Her breath recovered, Margaret got out of the squeaky chair, gave the cross on the wall a quick flick with her duster and went back to cleaning the desk. Still lying on top of it, after all these years, was the black leather family Bible, a biography of Margaret Thatcher and a copy of Burke. If only Mr Brooks had given her some small sign of approval, made her feel that she was more than fit to tie his shoelaces. How different was the man with the friendly dog! When Walter had spoken to her as if she was worth talking to, she had panicked. Was she foolish to think that he might find her interesting?

With Mr Brooks glowering his disapproval and the Lord's condemnation ringing in her ears, Margaret put on her coat and made her way to the Botanic Centre.

* * *

Rebecca pulled up in her four-by-four outside her father's house.

'Why do we have to visit Margaret?' Michael asked.

'Yeah, it's boring. I want to go home,' Martin said pouting. 'She cooks turkey every time.' Michael wrinkled up his nose.

Rebecca took out her lipstick and flipped down the sun visor to uncover the small mirror. In Rebecca's mind it wasn't make-up, it was ammunition.

'Sometimes you've got to put up with boring old people who've no one else to talk to about the boring things from their past,' she said into the mirror as she dabbed and poked at her face. She gave her lips a quick slick of red.

The kids didn't seem to be listening. 'Why do you put on make-up?' asked Michael.

'Because it can help girls who are still young and beautiful like Mummy to meet a special friend.'

'But why is Daddy not your special friend anymore?'

'Out of the car!' Rebecca snapped. She turned the ignition off, threw open the heavy jeep door and marched up to Margaret's front door. She noticed a 'For Sale' sign outside the house next door and licked her reddened lips.

'Come on, children – hurry up. You know what Margaret's like. She'll be panicking.' Well, she's no reason to panic as I'll deal with all her affairs, thought Rebecca.

* * *

Walter used his heart spray before hurriedly returning it to his pocket; Margaret was coming down the embankment. Although he couldn't see clearly at a distance, he could recognise people's gait: Margaret walked slowly with her head down. Ted confirmed it was

Walter's lady friend with a bark and wag of his tail. She went out of sight after she came through the main gate. Walter squinted in hopeful anticipation until he saw her reappear near to him.

They exchanged nods. Margaret sat at the end of the bench. Ted pawed her, then lay at her feet, and Walter saw that Margaret was as captivated by Ted as the dog was by her.

'Ted's never acted like that with anybody else. It's as if he's known you forever,' Walter said.

'What's Ted's story?'

'Ted's mother got in family way, father unknown. Once the owners realised she was about to have a litter they abandoned her at the side of the road. By the time a Good Samaritan found her, she was starving and covered in cigarette burns. They took her to an animal shelter where she had her pups. Ted was the runt. Luckily for me, no one wanted him and I found the wee dog in the cage. When he saw me he came over and wagged his tail and barked – we hit it off straight away.'

Margaret nodded.

'A dog like Ted always picks his own keeper,' Walter went on. 'My mother never wanted a dog, but she had been gone a long while when I met Ted so I didn't think it was disrespectful. I got him late in life and we've grown older together.'

'That's a beautiful story,' said Margaret smiling.

'We were both unwanted,' Walter said, gazing at the sheen of Ted's coat.

'I think Rebecca would put me in a home if she could,' Margaret blurted out.

'Rebecca?' 'My daughter.'

'And may I be so bold as to enquire if your husband is still ...?'

'He's passed ten years,' Margaret said sniffing.

'I'm sorry.'

'I can't pretend it wasn't hard. He was the only one who wanted me.'

'What?!' Walter jolted upright on the bench. 'I find that very hard to believe.'

'Maybe I *should* go into a home,' Margaret said under her breath.

'Personally, I wouldn't like to be in a home – and I've Ted. He's good company, and homes don't like pets. But you seem very independent and capable to me. Why would you need to go into a home?'

'My rock was Mr Brooks. With him gone, it's been difficult finding a purpose – a point to being me.' Margaret looked distant, yet said the words with such conviction that Walter had to restrain himself from placing a comforting hand on her shoulder.

'I felt – and in a strange way still feel – like that about my mother,' Walter said. 'She shaped me, taught me right from wrong. She taught me duty – the duty I owed her after she carried me in the womb, a duty I could never repay. Since she passed, my days are a bit like the studs in Ted's collar – each hard, cold and identical to the last.'

'But you and Ted are so ... nice, so very well suited,' Margaret said comfortingly.

'A dog's affection is always sincere, honest. Dogs bite their enemies and lick their friends. People, well ...'

Margaret shifted a little on the bench and said nothing for a moment. 'What did you do before retirement?' she eventually asked.

Walter laughed, but turned it into a cough. 'I worked in the Civil Service handing out forms all day and asking people to sign at the bottom. I might as well have asked them if they wanted chips with that. I was faceless. I had a routine. I arrived at ten to nine in the mornings and left at five in the afternoons. I had thirty minutes for lunch. Then I checked work that had already had been checked twice before. In the forty years I was there I never found one mistake.' Walter wrapped Ted's lead tightly around his hand.

'And you stuck at it?'

'Nameless, faceless, pointless though it was, I was contributing to my mother's life – putting food on the table, looking after her – and that kept me going. Then when I was told she needed twenty-four-hour care, I had no choice. It was my duty.'

'Duty was drilled into me too.'

Walter decided to take a risk. 'If I'm not being too forward could we meet again? I usually go for a cuppa on Sundays.'

'Next Sunday?'

'Yes, would that suit you?' Walter held his breath.

'No.' Her rejection was emotionless and blank.

'That's fine, Margaret. I'm sorry. I meant no offence. Me and Ted will bid you good day.' He staggered to his feet yanking a surprised Ted by the lead.

'It's just ...' Margaret was staring at his feet.

Walter hesitated.

'I'm ... oh I don't know ... I'm afraid,' Margaret said, wringing her hands.

Walter bowed slightly in her direction. 'If ever I've given you cause to be afraid I'm very sorry. It certainly wasn't my intention. We'll go.' But Ted stood his ground and refused to budge.

'It's just that I can hear Rebecca in my head. She'd say that Mr Brooks would be turning in his grave. My Rebecca is always right and whatever she doesn't know isn't worth knowing. And it would all go wrong anyway. I'm afraid you won't like me if you got to know me. And I so want you to like me.' Margaret poured it all out in a rush.

Walter laughed. He couldn't help himself. 'Oh, is that all? Listen, I'm just an insignificant old man, and it'd be a great pleasure to make your acquaintance. I don't know what kind of men you're used to, but I'm quite sure I'm not one of them. I'm a little bit afraid too, but I'm willing to give it a try.' He held out his hand.

Margaret smiled, and as she shook his hand she met his eyes.

Walter felt a warm glow inside.

After they parted, Walter walked carefully up the path through the park. His face had begun to sting with the cold when he left the shelter of the bench but he was smiling. For the first time in a long while Ted walked to heel, a youthful spring in his step.

Chapter 5

During the week, while Margaret was out doing her grocery shopping she stopped outside the hairdresser's. She looked at the beautiful young women with brightly coloured hair who appeared on the posters in the salon window. She touched her own dry, grey hair self-consciously. It had never occurred to her before to go to a hairdressing salon. She had always just used a bar of soap and had cut her own hair. Mr Brooks had thought shampoo, conditioner and hairdressers a 'fiddle'. But the salon was advertising perms, and she was somehow more interested now.

'Do you have an appointment, Mrs …?' asked a young girl when she entered the salon. It was empty of customers. The girl had blonde highlights and purple fingernails with glittering gold stars on them . She was pretty, but was heavily made up and wore a trashy-looking uniform. She reminded Margaret of the receptionist at her doctor's surgery, the one who looked at you as if to say 'you're old and a drain on resources so go die somewhere – cheaply'. The salon girl frowned as she looked at Margaret's unkempt, dull hair.

Margaret felt her confidence waning; then she thought of Walter and Ted. 'No, I don't have an appointment. But I really want to have my hair done – permed … and with a colour. Auburn!'

'If you'd like to make an appointment we could fit you in maybe in a few days?' The girl smirked.

Just then another lady, older with bright, friendly eyes and dressed immaculately in a manager's uniform, appeared. 'I can take you now. I'll make you ten years younger,' she said, smiling warmly.

Margaret smiled back. 'No, I'm happy at my own age, but thank you. I just want to look more … more presentable.'

'The lucky man won't know you,' said the lady, ushering her into a black leather chair.

Margaret blushed as she sat facing the mirror. She looked at her features; she was like the woman in Vera Drake. She had never thought anyone would look at her with any interest, but now she had a 'special' friend.

* * *

Rebecca didn't feel like making the boys' lunch that day. She had a bit of a hangover from the bottle of red wine she'd drunk the night before and the thought of even looking at food turned her stomach. I know, she thought, I'll take them round to Margaret's. She's always glad to see them. But Margaret hadn't answered her phone calls and Rebecca was getting cross. She coaxed the boys into the jeep and drove round to her father's house to find out what Margaret was playing at.

Outside the front door, Rebecca rummaged around in her handbag to find the key, the boys impatiently hopping from one foot to another.

'Mummy, I want to go home and watch CBBs,' Michael whined.

'So do I, Mummy,' chimed Martin.

Where's the bloomin' key? Rebecca hoped she hadn't left it back at her own house.

'I'm bored, Mummy,' said Michael.

'Mummyyyyyy,' whined Martin.

'Yes, yes – okay. We just need to make sure Margaret's not in any trouble. Why don't you both wait in the car?'

'Why Mummy?' they said in unison.

'Just do what Mummy says,' she snapped.

Grumpily they stomped back to the car, slamming the doors as hard as they could.

At last, Rebecca found the key tucked away in the corner of a pocket in her bag. It slipped into the lock and turned with a rusty click. Margaret was never usually out when she called, so she had

had no call to use the key before. It was much less effort to just ring the bell and have Margaret let her in.

Rebecca pushed the door open. 'Margaret? Margaret, where are you?'

She walked through the house room by room. Everything was as it should be – shabby and dilapidated. She became wary, expectant, even a little hopeful as she looked round the side of the bed and other places where Margaret might have fallen. Then she looked out of the front bedroom window and did a double take.

Someone who looked very like Margaret was walking down the street towards the house carrying Bonmarché shopping bags, only this Margaret was taller and walking without shuffling; she also had neatly permed, radiantly coloured hair. Rebecca clattered down the stairs and stood waiting at the front door, hands on hips, her cheeks crimson.

'Margaret? Is that you?' she called out. She was outraged. She felt like taking possession of the house straight away and leaving Margaret out on the street.

As soon as Margaret caught sight of Rebecca she began to shuffle again, prompting Rebecca to take advantage of the old lady's dwindling confidence. She blocked her way at the door.

'Margaret! Where have you been? I've been worried sick. I thought I was going to find you in a heap.'

'I was out doing some shopping.'

'And what, may I ask, have you done with your hair?'

Margaret put her hand to her head. 'I got a perm.'

'I can see that. What on earth possessed you?! And look at the colour of it! You were out having your hair done while my children were waiting to get something to eat.'

'I didn't know you were coming.'

'That's no excuse. You've been out of the house far too long. I've been calling you for ages. Maybe I should just leave you alone in future. There's no law to say I have to visit you. How would you manage then? You can't manage without me. Don't forget that.'

'I'm sorry.' Margaret dropped her bag at her feet. It was raining again, yet Rebecca still stood on the step, barring her way.

'You're always sorry.'

The rain was ruining her hair and Margaret began to cry. Her new-found confidence was being washed away with the rainwater in the face of Rebecca's unjustified anger.

Rebecca rolled her eyes and walked past Margaret to the jeep. One of the twins blasted the horn, seeming to mock Margaret as she struggled into the house with her bags of shopping. They got dropped in a corner where they would remain untouched.

* * *

Walter looked around his living room, which hadn't been decorated since his mother passed. While she was alive, he had never been himself, whatever that meant. He wasn't used to being 'independent'. His mother always knew what he shouldn't do but had never been very clear about what he should.

As he climbed the stairs, he realised that his ever-present mother disappeared from his mind whenever he was with Margaret. It made him feel both guilty and relieved. He was wheezing by the time he got to the top. He grabbed the banisters and paused for a moment. 'These stairs are killing me,' he said himself, before going into the bathroom. How could he even contemplate letting anyone take his mother's place? It felt like a betrayal of the person to whom he owed *everything*. It would not do. It really, really, really wouldn't do.

Ted wanted fed and was whimpering so loudly in the kitchen that Walter he could hear him from behind the bathroom door. When he had finished his ablutions, he made his way slowly back down the stairs again and went into the kitchen.

The dog woofed his appreciation and waited patiently while Walter took a tin of Chum from the cupboard, awkwardly cranked the lid open and scraped the contents into the bowl.

Ted sniffed the food carefully.

'No one's going to poison you, boy, that's for sure. You're as careful in life as me.'

Satisfied, Ted buried his nose in the food and gobbled it down hungrily, completely focused on his task.

Chapter 6

Walter had been counting the days until it would be Sunday again. Ted nudged his leg.

'Go and lie down, boy.'

Time was supposed to go faster when you were old, so why did it seem to be creeping along? Ted barked.

'Quiet,' Walter whispered. 'Quiet. What's got into you, boy?'

* * *

Margaret washed Michael's and Martin's PE kits. They had been playing for their school football team and no matter how hard she scrubbed she couldn't get the stains out. She still used a twin tub – Mr Brooks had refused to get one of the newer washing machines – but it was antiquated, much like herself, and wasn't very good at washing anything anymore.

She shivered. The Economy 7 heaters were on, but they were almost useless. They left her cold in winter, too warm in summer and the rest of the time struggling to pay the bill. This was the place she had spent the last forty years of her life and most likely where she would die, but more and more it resembled a prison.

As if mocking her, Cell Block H started on the black and white television, the old Australian programme opening with its romantic theme tune: 'He used to give me roses ...' At the word 'roses' she immediately thought of Walter and Ted, then of Mr Brooks. Her husband had once told a florist that Margaret's favourite flower was the cooking type. He'd laughed at his joke for weeks. She winced as she recalled it now. The theme tune seemed to get louder. 'Walter and Ted,' she said out loud as if weaving a charm.

Instantly the day seemed a little brighter; she didn't even feel as cold. She giggled, feeling like the schoolgirl she had never been allowed to be. Feeling cooped up, she picked up a woolly green jacket and left the house.

She walked down the familiar road without a headscarf hiding her hairdo and without any fear that something might go wrong. She felt invincible. She kept pace with a young couple who were walking their Alsatian. She looked at the dog and then at the couple and knew that Ted and Walter would be waiting for her.

* * *

Ted kept looking at the front door. He was very restless. He'd look at Walter with his big brown pleading eyes, then at the front door.

Walter stared at the picture of his mother. Sure Margaret wouldn't be at their bench, and anyway, even if she had gone today she wouldn't be there this late. Still, he stood up. Ted barked in anticipation. Much to the dog's delight, Walter put on his coat and picked up his black stick. He opened the door and together they walked down the tree-lined path that led over the embankment to the Botanic Centre, Ted tugging gently on his lead and Walter puffing on his inhaler so he could keep up.

* * *

Margaret and Walter arrived at the bench simultaneously. Walter was worried that she had been waiting and was just leaving.

'My apologies. I'm a bit late.'

Ted sniffed the bench uncertainly.

'I've just arrived too,' Margaret said smiling warmly.

They turned and walked towards Helen's café together, Ted enjoying taking his time for a good sniff along the way.

Helen was cleaning the windows and saw them coming. That's a relief, she thought to herself.

Walter and Margaret came in and sat quietly at a table in the café. The place seemed to be filled with a nervous silence. Like last time, it was empty except for a workman sitting at another table and

Helen herself. Yet the winter's sun gave the café an interesting glow that made everything feel like it had been cleaned and renewed.

Gradually, over two cups of tea, they began to talk.

'I feel different with you, Walter. I don't know why. It's as if you're a protective spirit.'

'Would love's young dream like a warmer for your pot?' Helen butted in.

Margaret blushed.

'Have we been here too long without ordering something else?' Walter asked.

Helen broke into a rapturous, hearty laugh. 'Well duckie, now you mention it …'

Walter smiled and picked up the laminated menu. 'Let's see – we're both going to have to have a fry-up!'

Helen put her hand into her pocket and brought out her order book. As she scribbled she said aloud: 'Two large fry-ups for table six.'

'My Rebecca doesn't approve of me eating things like fry-ups,' Margaret said. 'I've not had a fry-up in years. I've to cook turkey all the time.' 'I know. They're bad for you, aren't they. We really shouldn't! Walter said gleefully.

'We'd be two rebels!' Margaret exclaimed brightly.

'Yes, let's!'

'Yes!' Margaret echoed. Then almost immediately, she shrank back in her seat, tears gathering in her eyes. 'I thought I could meet you and get back in time to cook them their turkey. I don't even like turkey!' To Walter's relief she chuckled but quickly put her hand over her mouth as if shocked by the noise coming out of it. She took a linen hanky out of her bag and wiped her eyes.

Helen chortled and went off to cook their frys.

Walter watched Margaret laughing and crying at the same time and realised that he had feelings for this lady. Then when Margaret closed her eyes and sighed, he discovered a peacefulness inside him, like he had come home. Why had he never felt this before?

'I'd like to get to know you better,' he said to her, his knuckles white from clutching his tea cup.

'There's not much to me. I watch television a lot. I was watching Cell Block H before I came out, but I couldn't stick another moment of it today. The television was my husband's.' Darkness and fear clouded her eyes.

Ted scratched outside the door of the café to remind them he was still there. Silence descended again momentarily.

'My mother bought our first television,' Walter said eventually. 'My grandmother was so religious that when the pope was due to give his Easter message on television, she'd say "In the name of heaven, tidy the house – the pope's coming!".'

Then the darkness disappeared and Margaret laughed as they leaned together over the small square table.

'I'm afraid,' Margaret said at last.

'It's our time of life.'

'I'm afraid of being alone,' she said, sipping her tea. 'Yet I've been alone forever. When I'm alone I feel so weak.' She seemed surprised at her own openness.

'I got Ted and he changed everything,' Walter said. 'It might change for you too.'

'I feel as if my husband might not have been right about absolutely everything either, thinking about it now.'

'What shall we do?' Walter said, shocking himself with his question.

'Perhaps we need … I don't know … to make our own minds up.' Margaret seemed equally shocked at her suggestion.

'Could we be friends?' Walter asked tentatively, gripping the sides of the table with both his hands.

'Well … yes, I think we can,' Margaret said, daring to look Walter in the eye.

Helen set the fry-ups in front of them. Walter handed her some money.

Margaret opened her bag and produced a ten pound note.

Walter held his hand up. 'Please, Margaret, will you allow me?'

Margaret's eyes widened. 'Walter … you're such a … a gentleman! A perfect gentleman!'

Walter, unsure what to say, just smiled, hoping his few missing teeth weren't noticeable. He thought back to the last time he had offered to pay and her outright rejection of it. They had come a long way since then, further than his heart had dared hope.

They picked up their knives and forks and began to eat. Walter couldn't help watching Margaret – it was as if she was eating a four-course meal at an expensive hotel. In that moment, he felt so close to her and enjoyed her childlike sense of wonder. He knew this was the right moment.

'I've a surprise for you, Margaret … this very night. I've taken a liberty!'

'A liberty?'

* * *

They met again later that evening by arrangement. Margaret was wearing the same dowdy clothes and had the same downcast look, but something was different; there was some subtle change in the way she moved. Then he noticed that she wasn't wearing her wedding ring.

'Where's Ted?' Margaret asked, concern etched on her face. 'He's not sick, is he?'

'Ted's fine. He's safe and well and sleeping by the fire,' Walter said reassuringly. 'He didn't want to come tonight.'

'Oh, I hope it wasn't me that had that effect on him,' Margaret said clutching her bag tightly.

'No, I believe it was the effect you had on me!'

'Eh?'

'Come on, we need to get moving,' Walter said, changing the subject quickly. 'My poor arthritic legs don't move as fast as they used to!'

In their haste, Margaret's and Walter's hands accidentally touched and they both drew back as if they'd got an electric shock. It gave Walter goose pimples in the most delicious way and the lyric of an old song came to him: 'You never knew what place you took when you touched my hand.'

Walter led the way and they set off towards the river.

'I'm interested in architecture. Let's take a closer look at that building over there,' he said, smiling a little mischievously and pointing. He felt like a teenager again, he wasn't quite sure why. They crossed the road and went towards the domed Waterfront Hall.

'Gosh, there's an huge crowd there, Walter. I wonder what's going on. It's full of nuns and ladies almost my age. And look at the building! It's round and beautiful, like the table at Camelot. The story of King Arthur is the only book I can remember reading. I used to wish that a knight-errant that would come and rescue me. My mother and father read the newspapers but frowned on books. Mr Brooks discouraged reading too. He said that books should only be read for facts and since I couldn't even do my job at home there was no point in learning about faraway places. Oh, I wish I knew fancy words to express myself better.'

'I never heard anything described so beautifully! Would you like to take a closer look at the building?'

'Okay. But if there's something on perhaps we should stay away.'

'No one will mind us taking a closer look. Let me give you some boring facts about it,' Walter said, putting his glasses on and producing a leaflet. 'It was built in 1997 for the sum of thirty-two million pounds. There are two thousand two hundred and forty-one seats in it and it's based on the Berlin Philharmonic Hall. The dome of the building is coated in copper so it will turn green and resemble the dome of Belfast City Hall and other Victorian buildings in the city. But most importantly, older people often visit it.'

'It doesn't say that, does it?' She put her hand over her mouth and giggled.

Walter smiled, but when he saw her looking down at his shoes, he quickly produced a piece of paper, which he put into her hand – he didn't want to miss the moment. She looked down at the gold slip of paper.

'It's not more information about the building, is it?' she asked, peering at it more closely. Then she put one trembling hand over her mouth. 'Tickets for Daniel O'Donnell! Walter! You're the sweetest, most special – you're my knight-errant. A gentleman knight.' She stopped walking for a moment, trying to take it in. 'Will they let us in? It might not be for the likes of me.'

'Maybe you're right,' Walter said. 'It might not be for the likes of you.'

Margaret's head dropped.

'It might not be *good enough* for the likes of you,' Walter said laughing.

Margaret lifted her head and beamed at him.

They joined the queue. They were going somewhere exciting! While they waited, Walter reached into his pocket and from its depths produced a small box tied with a pink ribbon.

Margaret look startled.

He took her hand and tentatively placed it in her palm. At first, Margaret just stood there frowning at her trembling hand. Then slowly, her hand closed around the box and she blinked. Her eyes widened and pleasure spread across her face.

'Can I open it?' she asked excitedly.

'Of course you can. It's not a Christmas present!'

Carefully, she untied the pink ribbon, opened the box and took out a little golden bottle.

'Oh my goodness! Walter! Chanel perfume! For me?'

'You like it?'

He got the answer he hoped for in her eyes. She'd told him that for years, she had only smelled of lavender and that it made her feel as if she didn't exist. She would no longer smell of nothing; now she would smell like someone – like herself.

Walter's and Margaret's footsteps chimed in unison as they moved from the cold outdoors to the warm foyer.

'Did you know that Daniel once got a girl into trouble?' Walter said.

'No!'

'Yes, he told her mother that she smoked.' Somehow, Walter managed to keep his face straight.

Margaret laughed. 'I've laughed more in the past few weeks than I have in the previous seventy years combined, Walter. You're such a tonic!'

But Walter noticed a cloud passing across her face. 'What's wrong?' he asked.

'I just don't want it to end,' she explained. 'It's bound to, isn't it, and what will I do then? I feel like I'm Cinderella in the fairy tale … and you're my Prince Charming. It's even better than I ever could have imagined.'

The queue began to inch forward again and Walter kept his hand on Margaret's arm to make sure she felt safe. He was no longer cold, but delightful shivers were running up and down his spine.

'I'm just afraid of it turning midnight and me having to go back to the drudgery,' she said quietly.

They reached the cloakroom and Walter handed his coat to the man behind the counter. Margaret, watching him intently, took off her coat too and gave it to the man. In return, he gave her two tickets. Margaret reached for her purse but Walter placed a hand on hers and gently shook his head.

'But he's doing something for me,' Margaret muttered almost to herself.

'That's his job,' Walter explained. 'You keep our tickets safe in your bag. You're the kindest woman I've ever met … and I'm not saying that just because I'm over twenty-one,' he whispered loudly enough for her to hear.

They made their way to the main auditorium. Nearly every seat was already taken. An usher looked at their tickets and led them to their seats, four rows from the front on the left. Walter watched Margaret's eyes widen the closer they got to the front. He explained that the first three rows were always reserved for Daniel's family and friends, and people connected with the show, and hoped she wasn't disappointed with their seats.

'Disappointed? I'm … I'm … speechless,' she said.

Walter wondered just what Margaret had been allowed to do. Everything seemed so new to her. They had a good look around from where they sat. The place was packed. A nun in full habit looked down from one of the balconies.

Then the lights went down. He sneaked a peek at her and was amused to see the same expression on her face that women often wore at religious ceremonies. As the music began he couldn't help glancing at her again; this time he couldn't take his eyes away.

* * *

Margaret kept an eye on Walter too, mainly so she knew when to stand or sit, though she was too overwhelmed with everything going on around her to feel her usual self-consciousness. She didn't know of any of the songs but still hummed along as if partaking in prayer.

Walter seemed oblivious to Daniel O'Donnell. His hand accidentally brushed against Margaret's and she snatched hers away as if the ghost of her dead husband had slapped it. But then she reached out and grabbed Walter's hand as firmly as she could and held on to it this time.

'I've always dreamed of this!' she whispered.

'What, going to a concert?' Walter whispered back.

'No, holding someone's hand.'

Walter squeezed her hand by way of a reply. They were a couple, listening raptly as if the whole concert was for them.Mary Duff came on, wearing a beautiful formal sparkly evening gown, and duetted with Daniel. They seemed to have discovered the perfect symbiotic relationship, their voices complementing each other perfectly, their duet a call and response to the mystery of life. And when the music stopped, the auditorium erupted in clapping and loud cheers; Margaret forgot everything as she watched Daniel and Mary bow and smile and wave. Walter seemed to be just as engrossed.

Then something subtly changed. A spotlight was focused on an old women – older than Margaret – in the front row. Daniel introduced her as his mother, and she was greeted by round of roaring applause. His mother just sat there, looking like a rabbit caught in headlights. Margaret felt Walter wince. The spotlight fell back onto Daniel again who began singing, 'Medals for Mothers'. Walter clenched his fists.

Margaret turned to look at him. His eyes were filled with gloom, and tears were beginning to form. What had she done? It had happened as she knew it would – he had got to know her and didn't like her any more.

Hoping that there was some explanation that had nothing to do with her she asked him if he was all right. But he didn't seem to hear her. Margaret began to feel desperate. The voice in her head that had continually told her she was worthless and that had fallen silent since she met Walter now began shouting loudly again.

The crowd began clapping in time to the music; some held lighters aloft and others their mobile phones, hoping to capture the moment that was already etched forever on Margaret's memory for the best and worst reasons.

'It's late ...' Walter said stiffly to Margaret and let go of her hand.

Margaret shrugged and lowered her eyes.

Walter coughed. 'It's late and …' he said more loudly.

Margaret bit her lip.

'… Ted will be wondering where I am,' Walter said. He'd begun to sweat. 'It's almost midnight.' He offered his hand to her again, but this time to help her up out of her seat. Margaret couldn't take it.

They smiled and apologised quietly to everyone in their row as they pushed their way out to the aisle. She could see that Walter's eyes were filled with tears and knew that they were tears of pity for her. Why had she deluded herself? Why had he spoken such sweet words to her, words she had never hoped to hear, only to take them away again? It was so cruel. Out in the foyer they collected their coats in silence.

The doorman, who had been swaying in time to the music, looked at them in disapproval.

'What's the matter – can't hack the pace?' he asked as they made their way out into the cold night. The biting air and raw emotion struck together and Margaret pulled her coat tightly around her. Suddenly the old fear returned, along with the image of herself lying in a hospital bed, a 'nil by mouth' sign above her pillow and only Rebecca there waiting for her to starve to death.

Walter broke into her thoughts. 'Allow me to escort you home,' he said formally.

Margaret scowled. 'Don't bother. No one's going to attack someone with nothing,' she said and limped away from him, her legs stiff after sitting in the confined auditorium.

It's midnight and just like in the Cinderella fairy tale, he can see I'm no princess, she thought. I'm just me – worthless old me. She walked off, leaving him standing there. She didn't feel like going home so she headed in the direction of the Botanic Centre.

When she reached the bench – their bench – she fell down onto the seat with relief and, hunched over, put her head in her hands. She sat like that for a long time. Were all men like Mr Brooks? Maybe some were worse! At least Mr Brooks never feigned affection, not even on their wedding day. Pretending to like someone was surely the worst treachery. She was a joke to the Lord. She struggled to organise her thoughts. Walter has seemed so ... it had been like a beautiful dream. He'd been so nice and genuinely seemed to like her. He'd seemed sincere. Margaret sobbed.

Chapter 7

Walter unlocked his front door with a heavy clunk. His spirits had drooped lower than Ted's tail when the dog had been in the pound. He didn't even want to switch the lights on. The street lights had been too bright and unnatural on the route home and he longed for darkness. At least in the dark he could hide like the coward he was.

He called Ted. 'Sorry for leaving you, boy.' But where was Ted? Ted usually scampered over to greet him. Walter began to panic. 'Ted!' he called again loudly.

To his relief he felt Ted's wet nose press against his outstretched hand in the dark. The dog licked his hand but there was no welcoming bark.

'Okay Ted, don't tell me you need a walk now? Really? It's cold ... But I suppose you need to stretch your paws. You've been cooped up a long while.'

Ted gave a little yap. At least the dog seemed to know what it wanted.

Walter was deeply in need of tea with sugar, so he boiled the kettle and filled his flask with hot sweet tea. This had to have been both the best and worst night of his life. What had happened? He'd run away – that's what had happened. He was a coward, a chicken. Walter tried not to think about the hurt he had caused Margaret. Ted wagged his tail and pawed at him again.

'Okay Ted, where's your lead? I don't want to be anywhere but a dark room, but it would be nice to make someone happy tonight, even if you're the only one!'

Outside, the cold stung his face and he focused on reaching the Botanic Centre. The Centre itself would be closed to the public at that time but it was really the bench he was aimed for.

Ted strained at the lead, as if he was in a terrible hurry.

'Who's taking who for a walk?' scolded Walter, barely able to keep up.

Yet Ted pressed on – he knew he was going to his favourite place.

'Maybe I'll find a rock I can crawl under!' Walter muttered to himself.

Ted barked.

Walter often wondered just how much Ted understood. The dog's ears twitched as he listened to the silence of the streets – the sleeping houses full of sleepless people too worried about money to rest. They tried to shut it all out with satellite television that was no comfort when the bills came in. He knew because he was one of those people.

Walter's thoughts inevitably returned to Margaret. How had he managed to lose her before she had even come into his life properly. Causing someone pain seemed to be unavoidable – either he'd hurt her or he'd hurt himself. But he so wanted ... He didn't know what he wanted.

At the concert, he'd been overcome with feelings about his mother. His love for his mother was all-consuming, perfect, but ... what would his mother want if she were alive? 'I should be asking myself what I want,' he said to Ted. 'But sure there's no fool like an old fool, boy.' What had he done?

Margaret would be home by now, in bed and hopefully asleep, having already forgotten the events of the evening. He'd maybe send her a written apology. Yet how could he even begin? He was seventy-five years old and this was the worst thing he had ever done.

Walter saw the dimmed lights of the Centre in front of him. Ted began to pull harder; even the dog was behaving strangely tonight. Then as he got closer, he saw Margaret sitting on the bench. It took him aback. He hesitated for a moment, unsure if it would be better to retreat unnoticed or to sit beside her and try to explain something that he didn't understand himself. Ted made his mind up for him and barked his welcome.

Margaret looked up, mildly surprised to see them there, but without saying anything she stood up and walked past them back down the path. Before Walter could think of anything to say to her, two teenage hallions on bicycles appeared in front of them blocking the path.

Walter raised a quizzical eyebrow before drawing himself to his full height.

'That's him. That's him there!' said the youngster in the dark puffa jacket, jabbing his finger in Walter's direction. The teenagers bumped fists together and mumbled 'Res-pect.' The other kid, who wore no coat over his white hoodie, got off his bike and leaned it against a wall. He swaggered towards them; there could be no mistaking his intent.

In the blink of a moment, Walter stood in front of Margaret to shield her from attack. Ted stood courageously beside him, his fur spiked and his eyes narrowed; he was growling quietly.

Puffa got off his bike too and let it drop to the ground beside him, the clanging noise ringing out in the frozen air. He clenched his fist into a ball and stomped towards Walter. His jacket fell open to reveal a cheap red tracksuit underneath. He glanced back at his mate who urged him on. Puffa held himself as if he was weightlifter, but Walter could see that he looked more like an emaciated druggie.

Teenage troublemakers were always brave when they thought they had overwhelming odds stacked in their favour. It had been the same when Walter was at school, and even at work; there were little Hitlers on every street corner. Walter had met their type many times before. He rolled his eyes in disgust and shook his head. If these kids thought they were going to attack Margaret or him they had another thing coming to them.

Puffa came right up to Walter and putting his face really close, menacingly demanded, 'You slabbering?'

Walter held his eyes and said nothing. Puffa brought his fist up. 'You slabbering?' he repeated, his spittle spraying Walter's face.

'Sir, you're the one who's *slabbering*. Now, why don't you just let us go on our way.' Walter knew that good manners and reason would probably infuriate the youngsters more, but it was the only way he knew how to deal with confrontation at his age.

Puffa narrowed his eyes and jerked forward. Walter didn't flinch. Puffa looked at Margaret.

'Hey, you old cow, what're you lookin' at?' and before Walter could say a thing, Puffa turned back to him. 'Are ya slabbering now?' he asked and swung his fist, narrowly missing Walter's face.

Still Walter didn't move. Puffa's eyes widened; Walter held his gaze. Puffa looked back for reassurance. Hoodie waved his hand in encouragement but didn't make any attempt to join his accomplice.

'I'll knock you out,' Puffa said, not quite so sure of himself.

'Why don't you go home. Be off with you! Go on!' Walter ordered.

'What?'

'You heard!'

'What're you gonna do – throw your false teeth at me, you old gits?'

Walter heard a sharp intake of breath behind him. 'Apologise to the lady this minute,' Walter demanded angrily. 'I will not suffer her to be insulted.'

Puffa took a step backwards. 'Wha?' he said, looking puzzled.

'Oh sorry. Did I use too many big words for you? Say sorry to the lady, you hallion, then you can go!'

Puffa's eyes darted around nervously. He clearly hadn't anticipated this from an old man. 'You're mad, you are!'

Ted's head sank low and he snarled viciously; he was ready for anything.

Puffa took a step back 'You keep that mutt under control!'

Walter stroked Ted's head firmly. 'He doesn't answer to mutt. His name's Rambo.' Right on cue, Ted growled loudly again. 'He will take the appropriate action on my command,' Walter added fiercely.

Puffa eyed the two of them up; Walter could almost hear him think. Meanwhile, Hoodie had got back on his bike and was heading off in the opposite direction.

'Some friend he is!' Walter laughed. 'I suggest you follow him.'

Left on his own, Puffa seemed to shrink, his body hunching as if he was the old vulnerable one.

Walter knew that he had faced him down. 'Now apologise, sir!' he said and poked the teenager in the chest with his finger.

'I don't want any fights to start on account of me,' Margaret said over Walter's shoulder.

'Don't worry, Madam, they won't. This young person was about to prove himself and apologise. Weren't you?'

Puffa stared at the ground. 'Missus, I didn't mean to disrespect you.'

Walter shrugged. 'I suppose that'll have to do.'

Puffa turned and, grabbing his bike, scurried off to join his mate, a white ghostly figure looming in the darkness.

'You'll need eyes in the back of yer head, you crazy old twats,' Hoodie yelled at them. Puffa made an obscene gesture and the two of them rode off into the night.

For a moment, neither Walter nor Margaret nor Ted moved; it was as if they were rooted to the spot. Then Walter turned around. Margaret was as white as a sheet and looked as if she was about to collapse. Walter gently guided her back to the bench.

'Oh, how brave you were!' said Margaret. 'That's the bravest thing I've ever seen – better than the movies! You were like Clarke Gable or Errol Flynn or ... No one has ever defended my honour before!'

'Madam, they can have every breath in my body,' Walter said. Ted nudged his leg and Walter patted him. 'Ted is the bravest one. Lucky they didn't notice his teeth – most of them have fallen out! A bit like my own! ... Errol Flynn – really?' Walter was laughing, relieved it was all over and nothing serious had happened. 'Honestly, kids these days! They shouldn't have done away with National Service – that would give those kids something to think about. Teach them some manners too. Where are their parents or grandparents?'

Margaret laughed, this time without covering her mouth with her hand. 'It's just that you thought I was worth defending! I can't get over the fact that you risked your own safety for me! I'm amazed!'

Ted wagged his tail vigorously and it thumped, thumped, thumped against the bench. She certainly seemed to have brightened up a bit, but Walter was still concerned about her pallor.

'Better get you home, Margaret. I'll call you a taxi There's a phone nearby that automatically calls one.

'That's too extravagant,' she said. 'It's not far from here.'

But Walter was having none of it. 'Madam, I insist – and it's my treat. I'm sorry about the way I behaved earlier this evening. It's an old emotional wound that I'd like to tell you about some day. It would be the greatest honour of my life if you'd allow me to see you again.'

They set off along the path towards the phone. Walter took off his coat and draped it around her shoulders.

'You'll catch your death!' protested Margaret. 'You're such an old-fashioned gentleman.'

As they walked their hands touched, and rather than pull away, their fingers entwined. Fortunately, the taxi didn't take too long to arrive. The bald driver sounded the horn rudely, even though he knew they'd seen him, but Walter ignored him.

'It would be great to meet you again next Sunday at our bench. Would two thirty in the afternoon suit you?'

Margaret merely smiled and nodded. Walter slipped his coat back off her shoulders and put it on, swirling it around him like a cape. Ted wagged his tail and pawed at Margaret.

'I'd better go or he'll be charging extra,' Margaret said as she bent down to pat Ted on the head.

Walter opened the front door of the taxi for Margaret and she got in.

'Where are you for?' the driver demanded.

As Margaret told him, Walter handed him a ten pound note. 'Will that cover it?'

'Yes, that'll do it mucker,' the taxi driver said, saluting him with the tenner.

Walter knew he'd paid too much, but he didn't care; he just wanted to ensure that she got home safely.

'Make sure you wait until she gets in the front door,' Walter added.

'Will do,' the driver said.

'Safe home,' said Walter.

'You too,' she said. 'You too.'

'With this ferocious animal here to protect me, how can I go wrong?'

Margaret laughed and Ted barked as Walter pushed the passenger door closed.

Walter watched the taxi speed off under the glowering skies. He felt *different*. He looked down at Ted.

'Some people bring out the worst in you and some the best. That lady has made feel things I didn't know existed. I haven't had such a bad time … and such a good time since … ever.'

Chapter 8

Margaret had kept herself busy cleaning, dusting, hoovering, folding and ironing. She looked again at the bottle of Chanel that Walter had given her. It had been taunting her all week as it sat on her dressing table. What should she do with it? She'd put it in the bin several times already. Where could she hide it? She put it in the cupboard of her bedside table, but she'd forgotten that the door was loose and it fell off and hit her foot; she lifted her eyes to heaven in supplication.

She glanced at her watch. It was almost time to leave. As she anticipated seeing Walter again, she decided to dab a little of the perfume behind her ears and on her wrists. The smell was divine! She checked herself in the mirror, pushing back a few stray strands of hair, put on her coat and scarf and left the house.

She walked briskly to their bench, the autumn sun briefly warming the footpaths as if to show her the way. Ted and Walter were already there waiting for her, the remnants of the last shower glistening like diamonds on the cast iron frame of the bench. Walter stood up as soon as he saw Margaret and waited for her to sit down before he resumed his seat. He opened his flask and poured her a beaker of hot tea.

'What about this weather?' Walter began. 'It's getting worse. I worry what kind of environment we are leaving the next generations.'

Margaret smiled. 'It's now that I'm worried about. My Rebecca and her family. I worry that she's drinking too much … and about all the other problems she has. I wish there was more I could do, but it's just me by myself. Just me.'

'If I may be so bold – from what you've told me, I think your Rebecca can look after herself!'

Margaret wrung her hands and frowned. She didn't much like what Walter was implying about her daughter. 'Rebecca's a good person. She looks out for me ... and ... where would I be without her?'

'You're more honest than that!' Walter said, immediately putting his hand over his mouth.

Ted's ears drooped and he set his chin on the ground. The air around them seemed to drop a few degrees. Margaret emptied what was left of her tea to the side of the bench and watched it seep away into the earth.

'Rebecca's always right,' she said. It was a homily she repeated often. 'Rebecca's always right. She kills herself every day for those boys and for me. It can't be easy for her on her own. I'm sorry, but it isn't ... I'm sorry. She's everything to me and since Mr Brooks and I ... I was a disappointment as a wife and a mother. I never knew how to talk to her. I got thrown in at the deep end. And I don't think that ... If I lost her and my grandchildren I don't know what I'd do.'

Walter looked puzzled but refused to let it go. 'Who are you trying to convince? The Margaret I know has a core of steel when she can see things the way they are. You deserve all of God's blessings, especially that of love.'

The words were like hot knives to Margaret and she could feel her eyes fill with tears. 'Love is for other people, not for me!' she said trying hard not to cry. 'You're going to get to know me, and then become bored with me. Maybe the reason you're talking about Rebecca like that is because you're already tired ...'

From the expression on Walter's face, he really didn't understand.

'And what about your mother?' she went on. 'How would you feel if I said things about her?' Then she too put her hand over her mouth. 'Sorry, I've never spoken back to anyone before.' She knew that what she said had hit home.

'My mother graced this earth and tried to do everything she could for me,' he said in a high thin voice that she barely recognised. 'She did more for me than ... more than anyone else has or ever will.' She could see the tears prick his eyes.

Blinking hard, Margaret stood up, handed Walter his cup and walked away down a shadowy path. He'd definitely never want to speak to her again after that.

* * *

Ted tugged at his lead wanting to follow Margaret, but Walter felt much too wounded to comply. Was she suggesting that he was a mummy's boy, at the age of seventy-five? Ted pulled harder.

'Ted,' he scolded. 'Ted!' He pulled hard on the lead. 'I've never heard the like,' he said to himself. 'I will not tolerate any kind of slur on Mother.' Walter stood up and went to walk off in the opposite direction to Margaret but found that Ted refused to move. 'What's wrong with you, silly dog!' He yanked on the lead but Ted lay on the ground, head between his paws, ears flat.

'Sausages at Helen's!' Walter said, confident that that would do the trick.

But Ted didn't budge.

Walter sat down again on the bench. Eventually Ted shook himself and pulled Walter up and in the direction of home. Ted's tugs on the lead were not reassuring but painful and Walter was reminded yet again what it was to be old; worse still, to be old and full of regrets. He peered into the distance searching for a glimpse of Margaret but knowing she was long gone.

Walter walked home slowly, both he and Ted disinterested in their surroundings. People came pouring out of a church onto the street. He noticed a woman with her back to him and knew it was Margaret!

'Margaret!' he called. 'I'm so …'

The woman turned around and it wasn't Margaret at all. Walter's gaze dropped.

Then he glanced across the road and recognised Margaret's unmistakable shuffling walk. He crossed the road quickly, a car slowing and blasting its horn at him.

'Margaret?' he called, but the lady did not turn round and to his despair he realised that she wasn't Margaret either.

Then another lady with hair like Margaret's stepped out of a side street. Just as Walter was about to call out another woman rounded the corner wearing a coat like Margaret's. He sensed someone glaring at him and felt sure it was Margaret. But when he turned round he saw a child of around twelve years old peering at him out of a passing bus. He'd never experienced anything like this before.

'What's happening?' he asked the sky in despair.

Eventually he and Ted made it home, the place that had held the world at bay for decades. It was his mother's house, the place where he had been born, where he had played as a child and the place where he would die.

He made himself a cup of tea and sat beside the fire, Ted at his feet, looking into the dying embers. The memory of his argument with Margaret repeated in his head, the way the castor oil his mother had insisted he take had. Of course he would've liked to have a relationship with a lady, but mostly he felt resigned. Relationships weren't everything, and anyway he had Ted. His mother had taught him to be self-sufficient, but she hadn't taught him what to do when he felt the absence of human companionship.

Walter looked around the sparsely decorated room. Only one photograph hung on the wall, a picture of his mother holding him as a baby. She was standing on the balcony of a hotel in some sunny spot. He took the photograph down and wiped it carefully with a cloth. He needed to put it somewhere more appropriate; it needed to make way for a new image. He loved his mother, but he realised he loved Margaret differently ... more. He said it out loud – 'I love Margaret ... I really love her!' – and somehow it made it more real.

He leaned over and ruffled Ted's fur. What was he to do about Margaret? He switched on the telly to distract him, but it was tuned to a love story in which a young man relentlessly pursued a woman whom he had lost. Walter felt the tears prick his eyes. If he didn't take some kind of action, he would be tortured by every love song, every romantic movie, and each time he went down to the bench at the Centre. He refused to take these regrets to his grave!

'Time waits for no man,' said Walter, vaguely remembering some proverb or other. 'And we're not getting any younger, are we Ted!'

Then he suddenly saw things clearly. Yes he loved his mother, but life was for the living not the dead. Life without Margaret would be like a living death. 'But it'll take more than perfume … or flowers or chocolates to win her round!' Walter had just had a brilliant idea.

Ted looked round at him quizzically and pawed at Walter's foot.

'Sometimes I think you understand every word,' Walter chuckled.

Ted wagged his tail.

Grabbing his stick and Ted's lead he put on his coat and walked out the front door. Maybe he wouldn't be able to get the things he needed; maybe Margaret would reject him utterly; but surely being alive meant more than just breathing – it meant taking a few risks.

Walter walked down the familiar street and went into the supermarket. The lady at the checkout was bemused by his purchases, but happily helped him put big batteries into the back of his new portable stereo.

It didn't take Walter long to find her house. It had clearly been a grand building once, but was now falling into decay and ruin. He walked in through the gates and stood at the front of the house trying to choose the best place to stand. He set the stereo down, inserted the CD, turned the volume up and pressed 'Play'. Within seconds, Brenda Lee was telling the entire street that he was sorry, that he had been a fool, that he'd been too blind to see.

Margaret peeped out through the blinds of a downstairs room. When she saw it was Walter she flung the window wide open.

'Walter! … Are you drunk?'

'I couldn't find a Mexican band to play outside your window, but this is much better,' Walter said. 'We've been fools, Margaret. Can you forgive me?'

Margaret laughed. 'I suppose I'd better invite you in for Ted's sake. He needs a sausage and a bowl of milk before he catches his death!'

Ted barked his approval.

'Old fool!' Margaret muttered, smiling, as she closed the windows. Minutes later she appeared at the front door. 'And what if the neighbours complain?' she went on, blushing in the most charming way. 'But you're so … what's the word?'

'Cold?'

'No – romantic! You're mad. You're a loon! You're … wonderful! You're the most wonderful person I've ever met. Hurry inside or someone will see you!'

Walter and Ted walked into the warmth of the house. 'The neighbours don't pay your rent do they?' Walter asked.

'No.'

'Well then – let them talk!'

'Oh, Walter! Walter! Have you forgiven me?'

'It's me who needs forgiveness!'

'I'll knock the kettle on!' said Margaret hopping from one foot to the other. I think we need to have a good chat.

Walter was about to draw her close when the phone rang.

Margaret stared at it as it rang a few times. 'It might be an emergency. I better get it,' she said and picked up the receiver, at the same time saying to Walter 'What did you want to tell me?'

Then she spoke into the phone: 'Hello? … No, Rebecca, there's no one here … I was talking to myself … I know you're not surprised …' Margaret turned to look at Walter and shrugged.

Walter, crestfallen, lifted Ted's lead and guided him back out the front door again. Margaret mouthed 'Sorry' at him as he left.

Chapter 9

Seven o'clock on Saturday evening and Rebecca sat with her elbow on the table and her fist pressed against her cheek, pondering poor old Margaret's future. It must be lonely for her in that big house all by herself with nothing to look forward to.

Rebecca fancied a night out. She hadn't had a good night out in ages. She looked in her purse. She could stock up on cash from her credit card, and Margaret could look after the twins for the night.

'Kiddies! Car!' shouted Rebecca

* * *

Margaret quickly fixed her hair in the hall mirror as she rushed to answer the door to her unexpected visitor. She wanted to say sorry to Walter properly.

Rebecca's eyes widened as she watched Margaret's face collapse with disappointment when she opened the door.

'Oh dear!' said Rebecca. 'Sorry to disappoint! Who were you expecting?'

'It's just that it's a Saturday and …' Margaret swallowed.

'Yes, it's Saturday. What difference does that make to you?' Rebecca gripped one twin in each hand. 'Your babysitting skills are required tonight. Now Margaret, I'm trusting you with my babies, so don't let me down.'

'I don't feel well,' Margaret said, looking at the ceiling where a stain made her wonder if she should decorate.

Rebecca shook her head sadly. 'That's terrible! Well, they can keep an eye on you then. You'll look after Margaret, won't you?' she said, turning to the twins.

The boys nodded. They were well wrapped up in thick coats, and woolly hats and scarves. Margaret couldn't help noticing

Rebecca's outfit: a remarkably short dress that more closely resembled an oversized belt. Margaret glanced back to the hall to check the time. She'd forgotten the clock was still being cleaned.

Suddenly, Rebecca looked at her suspiciously. 'Do I smell Chanel?'

Margaret couldn't look her in the eye and found herself clenching her fists. 'Oh, it must be the new polish I'm using.'

Rebecca frowned and then smiled. 'Good to hear you're keeping yourself busy around the house. Anyway, I'll be back tomorrow morning. So I'll see you then, my dumplings.' She kissed both the twins on the cheek, which made them scrunch up their faces, and they walked off up the hall.

'All their things are in Father's bedroom wardrobe,' Rebecca went on. 'I'm going to get myself a man tonight, so I might be back later or maybe tomorrow. Don't be giving them anything unhealthy for breakfast … Okay boys,' she called, 'look after Margaret. Make sure she doesn't do anything naughty!'

The twins nodded solemnly. Rebecca waved to them and slammed the front door behind her. A few seconds later, they erupted with noise and began jumping up and down on Margaret's settee.

'Careful, you might hurt yourselves!' Margaret shouted, but she knew they weren't listening.

She sat on the stairs with her head in her hands as Michael and Martin chased each other around the house for what seemed like hours. Eventually she heard their footsteps slowing on the landing and the sound of the bathroom door closing. Shortly afterwards, they went quiet. Margaret was filled with dread – silence usually meant that they were up to something. Then there was a splattering sound as one drenched toilet roll after another came flying down the stairs and splatted all over the place. Water splashed everywhere, and big gobs of soggy pink toilet paper clung to the floor and walls. Giggling loudly, Michael and Martin stuck their heads over the banister to admire their handiwork.

Margaret didn't move. She clasped her knees tightly to her chest and wished Walter was there.

* * *

Rebecca strode into the bar, the place where she'd first met Blake in the 1990s. Blake had taught her that relationships were about power and control. But tonight, she had decided, she was going to find someone whom *she* could control.

She surveyed the bar and, thinking of Blake and his proclivity for young woman, picked out two young men sitting at one of the small tables in the corner. They looked like they might be interesting. Her purse was bulging with cash – she'd maxed out her credit card, which she'd been using lately to pay the mortgage. Ah well, she'd worry about that later. She was determined to have a good time tonight, and making sure the guys knew she had plenty of money would help.

* * *

Several hours later, Rebecca was sitting on the toilet floor of the bar. The world was spinning, and not just because she'd had too much to drink. They'd called her a pensioner! an old doll! a has-been! Why, just a few years ago men had been willing to humiliate themselves to get her attention! Blake had been lucky!

She threw her cocktail glass, containing the remnants of a Kick in the Balls, at the toilet wall, the glass splintering all over the floor and the cocktail seeping into the tile cracks and staining her dress. She'd nothing to show for the night except an empty purse and a stain. She got on her knees and began to pray, but between the throbbing music coming from the bar and the drink, her words got mangled as they left her mouth: 'Hail Father, be in heaven, be blessed, a fat man in a needle, a poor thief …'

She gave up and staggered back to her feet, only to find herself confronted by a bedraggled drunk woman. Why was this old slapper staring at her? She'd be wearing her drink if she didn't stop eyeballing her! She wasn't in the mood for this. Rebecca spat at the old crone, and as the gob hit the mirror she recoiled in horror. Was she turning into Margaret? She tried to smile at the bedraggled woman in the mirror, but the old bint stared back, unfriendly and unforgiving. Rebecca almost slipped on the remains of the cocktail.

Propping herself against the sink, she rummaged in the darkest recesses of her handbag and produced a bottle of pills. She had a few left. Diazepam: Mummy's little helpers; Rebecca's little helpers; they helped her with everything. She lined the pills up in a row on top of the sink.

'I'll do it. I'll do it. I will,' she said to the old cow in the mirror.

She lifted one of the pills, put it in her mouth and swallowed, retching a little as the pill stuck in her dry throat. Eventually it went down. She found herself studying her bling – a gold cross that hung around her neck and swung from side to side like a metronome, keeping time with her heartbeat (thump, thump, thump), and a brooch that was pinned to her dress. Clumsily she prised the brooch open so she could see the photograph inside – the twins when they were babies. She just stood there, staring at herself in the mirror.

Suddenly she tore the gold cross from her neck and threw it into the sink. The Lord had done her no favours. It jangled as it hit the ceramic basin; she watched it slither towards the plug hole. She turned on both taps and washed it away as if it was a bug. The Lord was indifferent; Blake was indifferent; everyone was indifferent. There was no arguing with indifference. Only her children loved her.

'For them,' she said, 'For my boys. I'll never beg again, not to anyone – not God, not Blake!

Slowly, her tears of self-disgust were replaced by tears of anger. She gripped the sides of the sink, her rage keeping her steady. Margaret was to blame. If Margaret had been any kind of example, then Rebecca would have had a better upbringing. She should have had the things that she made sure her own children had. She'd go naked herself sooner than make her children go without. Why hadn't Margaret done the same?

If Margaret hadn't fainted when her father had had his heart attack, she'd have been able to phone for help and he'd still be alive. And if her father was still alive she wouldn't have married the first powerful man she met. And if she hadn't married Blake she wouldn't have been in this bar on her own. And if she hadn't been in this bar then she wouldn't have had to face such a cruel rejection. So, Margaret was to blame for everything. It was all Margaret's fault!

She'd been too kind to Margaret and Rebecca decided right there and then that that was going to change. She fixed her hair in the mirror, tidied her clothes, put the pills back in her bag and left.

She staggered out of the bar and into the cold night, wrapping her Jaeger coat around her. She staggered back to Margaret's, tottering on her high heels, her head woozy, and wished the winter would end. But I can't beg the weather for mercy any more than I can beg Blake, she thought. As she passed a black taxi rank, a driver wound down his window and yelled, 'Need a taxi, love?'

Rebecca shook her head.

The driver, an incredibly fat man, stuck his big round head out and called after her, 'It's not safe, love! You could be attacked or somethin'!'

'Chance'd be a fine thing!' she mumbled.

It was Blake or nobody for her. No one would love her except Blake. He was her last chance; he was the last man in the world. The drink and the sobering night air allowed her to look in the place that she was always afraid to look and loneliness stared back.

She wanted to go home and take a shower so hot that it melted the flesh from her bones and purged her clean. But she needed to give Margaret a piece of her mind, tell her what her upbringing had brought her to.

When Rebecca got to Margaret's she hammered the door with the giant iron knocker. She kept hammering and hammering. Eventually Margaret opened an upstairs window.

'Who's there?' she called out. 'Who

d'ya think?' Rebecca shouted.

Margaret quietly closed the window and a few minutes later appeared at the front door. Rebecca nearly pushed her over as she rushed into the warm house. Margaret looked ridiculous in fluffy pink slippers and tatty blue dressing robe, her hair tucked up inside a brown hair net. Margaret closed the front door and shut out the world once more.

'The twins! Give me my babies. Hurry up!' Rebecca demanded.

Margaret put her finger to her lips. 'They're sleeping in the spare bedroom. I think maybe they should be left the night. You can have my bed and I'll make do on the sofa,' she whispered.

'Since when did you tell me where and when?' Rebecca rattled her car keys above Margaret's head as if she were a jailor.

'I don't think you should be driving,' Margaret said.

'What did you say?'

'I don't think … I don't think you should drive.' Margaret's voice trembled.

'Did I ask what you thought? … Well, did I?'

Margaret snatched the keys from Rebecca and clutched them tightly. 'You're not driving with the twins.'

Rebecca swayed on her feet. 'How dare you tell me what I can do with my own children. I'm a far better mother than you ever were. Sure you never even learned how to drive … you took me nowhere. And how dare you suggest that I'd do anything to jeopardise my kids' lives.'

Margaret walked off towards the kitchen, Rebecca following her as she scolded. But Margaret still refused to surrender the car keys.

Rebecca raised her fist over Margaret's head; Margaret closed her eyes. 'What happens to me isn't important,' Margaret said, 'but I won't let you take the twins – not while you're in that state!''You're to blame! It's your fault! All of it! You cow!' Rebecca screamed at her.

Michael called from upstairs: 'Mummy?'

'What's going on Mummy?' yelled Martin.

The boys ran down the stairs, across the old brown carpet and into the kitchen where Margaret stood shaking and white. Rebecca lowered her fist.

Michael pointed at Margaret. 'Say sorry, Margaret! You've made Mummy all upset!'

'Yeah, no one talks back to Mummy!' Martin chimed in.

There was silence. Margaret said, 'I'll make you a nice cup of tea, and give the boys some milk. And if you like I'll call you a taxi. I can give you the money for it.'

Rebecca looked dazed for a moment, then she stared at her own fist. Unclenching it, she walked over to the twins and hugged them.

'I don't know what I would do without you both,' she said. 'I just don't know.'

She sent them upstairs to get dressed. Rebecca took the money from Margaret and once the boys were ready, they headed off into the night towards the nearest taxi office. But once they got there, she slipped the cash into her pocket.

'It's clearing up. Let's walk instead,' she said to the twins.

* * *

Rebecca tossed aside her coat and got into bed without washing or undressing. Michael and Martin jumped into bed with her too. They were cold. If they fell ill it would all be Margaret's fault. She hugged them both as they lay beside her.

'You're hugging too hard, Mummy,' Michael complained.

'You look like you're sick, Mummy,' Martin observed.

'Mummy's fine, my pigeons. Mummy is going to be just fine,' she mumbled, as she drifted off to sleep. Drink or no drink, she was still a good mum. More than could be said for Margaret. Margaret was going to pay. And it would cost a hell of a lot more than just money.

* * *

On Monday morning Rebecca was wakened by the doorbell ringing. Her head was pounding; she'd knocked back a full bottle of cheap red wine the night before to take the edge off her hangover. Now her hangover had a hangover.

At the front door, the postman offered her his pen to sign for a letter. It wasn't a gift. It was something she had been dreading for a while: a red Final Notice. Final Notice. Final.

The arrears had been accumulating and because of the economic depression, the house was in negative equity so she couldn't borrow against it. She took out the cash she had in her purse and counted it. She didn't have any more the second time she counted it.

The money she had got for the clock wouldn't be enough. It would barely cover the children's school uniforms and a month's mortgage. She'd no more credit left on her cards. She thought about her father's desk.

She flicked open the glossy *Antiques Valued* magazine, filled with hope, looking for inspiration. In her mind's eye she went through every room in her father's house trying to hit on something else of value. It was no good; she had already taken everything – except her father's desk.

She had had it valued twice already; it was worth at least fifteen thousand pounds. She did some mental arithmetic; it would give them six months reprieve. Six months of security for Michael and Martin. As her father used to say, 'It would keep the wolf from the door.'

It wasn't as if the desk belonged to Margaret. It had been her father's. She had more right to it than that silly old cow. And what difference did it make anyway? What use was it to anybody just sitting there gathering dust? It was part of *her* inheritance, not Margaret's. She decided she would pay Margaret a little visit the following Sunday. Just the thought of it made her feel better.

Chapter 10

'All my friends have Adidas Crazy Lights. I need them, Mummy,' Michael pleaded.

Martin pulled her arm. 'If Michael's getting them, then I want them too.'

Rebecca bit her lip. She found it so hard to say no to them. She wondered how much two pairs of Adidas Crazy Lights would cost.

'Please, Mummy. Say yes!'

'Yes, yes. Please, Mummy. Pretty please with sugar on top!'

Rebecca had decided that the old desk could do with a thorough clean and intended calling at the house. She wasn't a tyrant; she would give Margaret plenty of notice that she was 'restoring' her father's desk. After the way Margaret had behaved about the car keys, she was in no position to argue. When Rebecca had called back the next day to pick up the car, Margaret had been very rude to her. She'd claimed she had a migraine, but that was no excuse for such rudeness, Rebecca thought.

The smell of lavender permeated the air from her oil burner. The scent was supposed to relax her, but all it did was remind her of Margaret. If the old woman could suddenly afford an expensive new hairdo and new clothes, she could afford to help Rebecca and the children. It was her father's desk, her father's house; she owed Margaret nothing. Suddenly, she had a taste for overcooked turkey with too much sage in the stuffing.

'Children, we're going to visit Margaret,' she announced.

'Oh no, Mummy! Not again,' Martin said pouting.

Michael thumped the glass tabletop. 'I'm going to run away and not come back.'

'Look, if you want those Adidas shoes then you have to do as I tell you. Margaret will cook dinner and we'll eat it and make her feel important. Then she'll give us grandad's desk for restoration.'

'Her food's stinking!' said Michael picking his nose.

Rebecca slapped his hand down from his face. 'Stop it. That's a terrible habit! You'll make your nose bleed.' Rebecca lay back on the recliner. 'It's our duty,' she said sanctimoniously.

'I want Call of Duty for the Playstation. I don't want a boring old desk!' Michael said sulkily.

Rebecca took a deep breath while Michael and Martin struck her feet with their toys.

* * *

The first thing Rebecca noticed as she let herself into Margaret's house was the absence of the smell of cooked turkey. Had something happened to the old cow at last? Margaret wouldn't dare be late with the dinner, especially after the way she'd behaved last week. Rebecca was sure she'd made her displeasure known. She walked on into the house and stood still.

'Michael! Martin! Wait in the car,' she called back over her shoulder.

With tuts and moans they stomped over to the car. When she heard the slam of the car doors she steadied herself.

'Margaret!' she called, walking up the drab hallway. 'Margaret?' She went into the living room. She could see from behind that Margaret was sitting in her armchair; the television was on. Was she dead? Rebecca moved silently across the floor and bent down to look. Suddenly Margaret caught sight of Rebecca and jolted, which in turn made Rebecca jump. No, she wasn't dead … yet.

'Rebecca! Oh, I'm sorry,' Margaret said, her hands held up as if Rebecca was pointing a gun at her. 'I didn't think you were coming. Are you here for dinner? You usually call before you come. And it's much later than usual.'

'What? Are you telling me that me and the children are going to have to wait for something to eat?'

'Yes,' replied Margaret. She sat back in her chair.

'What?!' Rebecca could hardly believe what she was hearing. The impertinence. 'How dare you speak to me that way! You need to show some respect!'

Margaret didn't drop her head.

'Good grief! What would Father say if he was still here? I'm glad he's not able to see this!' Rebecca yelled.

This time Margaret's head did drop.

Rebecca breathed a sigh of relief. There was the old Margaret. She didn't know what had got into her lately.

'Right, well, since it'll take ages to prepare we'll give dinner a miss this week. What I really came round for was to do you a favour and get that old desk in the study out of your way. I'm going to get it restored. Some men will be here to pick it up tomorrow, but I thought you'd want to clear all the clutter out of it first.'

Margaret shrank back into her chair.

* * *

Walter knew something was up by the way Margaret was walking. It was all he could do to wait for her to come round the path. It was Sunday 13th and he was superstitious. What bad luck there was he could take, so long as Margaret was okay.

Margaret didn't meet Walter's eyes when she arrived, but she sat at the opposite end of bench as usual. She seemed very downcast. Walter waited for a moment before speaking; whatever was troubling her was bound to have to have something to do with Rebecca. Ted pulled his ears back and whined gently as he lay at Margaret's feet.

It had started to rain quite heavily and there was a strong wind whipping around them. But they were sheltered on their bench, protected from the worst of the storm.

'Oh, Walter!' Margaret said eventually. 'She wants the desk. The desk where ... oh Walter! What choice do I have?' She went on to tell him how much the desk had meant to her husband.

Walter felt like asking what the desk meant to *her*, not her husband, but instead said, 'You must tell Rebecca how you feel.'

'If I don't let her have the desk, she'll never visit me again and I'll never see my grandsons … and then I'll be totally alone.' Margaret began to cry quietly.

'You would not be alone, Madam,' Walter said firmly.

'Mr Brooks …' Margaret began.

'Mr Brooks?'

'My departed husband, Mr Brooks told me I wouldn't manage.'

Walter wondered what kind of relationship Margaret and her husband had had if she had to refer to him by his formal title. He wouldn't have been surprised if she had had to call him 'Mr Brooks, sir.'

Margaret explained that her husband had always told her that she wasn't smart enough or good-looking enough to survive on her own. She had given all she could to Rebecca and when she couldn't give any more, Rebecca had taken. But surely Rebecca knew what this desk had meant to her father and wouldn't let it out of the family.

Walter had heard enough to know that Rebecca would take until there was nothing left, and he was pretty sure Margaret knew that too. He was experiencing an unfamiliar feeling – might it be jealousy? of a dead man? – but his overriding emotion was one of protectiveness. Walter breathed deeply.

'I can't advise you, but I can be there for you. If you like, Ted and I can call at your house tomorrow to see how you are. Dependability is one of my few remaining vices.'

Ted wagged his tail in agreement.

Margaret sat quietly for a moment before she replied. 'Thank you, Walter. That would be very helpful. I think sometimes that God sent you here – that he's heard all my prayers.'

Walter blushed. 'It was my prayers that were answered, not yours!'

* * *

Later, at home, Margaret thought about Walter and Ted as she pulled on her yellow gloves. She was about to do something that she dreaded, but thoughts of her two new friends kept her going. She drew herself up and picked up a duster and a can of furniture polish.

Margaret entered the study with reverence, like a worshipper of some primitive god who demanded ever more sacrifice over the years. Confronting her as soon as she went in was the desk, its dark oak glowering at her from the far side of the room, daring her to touch it. She paused, then fixed the image of Walter and Ted in her mind and began to polish. She was polishing so hard it made her breathless and she coughed.

Now there could be no more excuses or distractions. It was time to open the desk. She turned to the oak bookcase containing a row of dull hard-backed books about accountancy, her husband's career, that were completely out of date now and had no value whatsoever. She knew where he had hidden the key and braced herself to commit the crime. She was just cleaning, she thought, cleaning.

She kept the gloves on, like a thief being careful not to leave fingerprints, and pulled a Bible off the shelf – except this wasn't God's holy word, but a hollowed-out book that held the key to her husband's most intimate belongings. She took the key and thrust it into the lock on the desk's main drawer; after taking a deep breath she tried to turn it. But the lock was stiff and she couldn't get the key to turn. She got a tea towel to give her a better grip and eventually, with a sigh of relief, she heard the sharp click as it unlocked.

She squeezed her eyes shut, pulled open the drawer and opened her eyes again. Inside, it was a filthy mess. She stood for a long time just staring at the jumble of papers crammed in there. Eventually she began to sift through it all, reading documents in the hazy light cast by the bulb in the ceiling, trying to figure out what was important and what could go in the bin. Then her eyes widened as she read a bank statement, which detailed large payments to private accounts. That's when she found the photographs.

At first she thought it was someone else's wedding, then she recognised a youthful Mr Brooks as the groom. But it wasn't her who was the bride. Holding onto Mr Brooks's arm was a young a beautiful woman, some other woman Margaret had never seen before. Both of them were smiling and gazing lovingly into each other's eyes.

Margaret collapsed on her knees, the papers of her late husband lying scattered around her. Her tears stained the bank statement and made the wedding photographs blister. They didn't stop the bride from smiling or wipe the familiar smug look from the groom's face.

After some time, Margaret sat up and looked again at the photograph of the other woman, this time marvelling at the bride's beauty, the happiness that radiated from her on her wedding day as she stood there in her perfect white dress. Mr Brooks face was lit up with a smile the likes of which Margaret had never seen him wear. She was drawn to the woman's platinum wedding ring. It had been her mother's ring and Mr Brooks had insisted that she'd lost it.

She pulled herself to her feet and walked to the mirror. She had always been reluctant to have mirrors in the house but this one had been her mother's, so as a compromise, she'd turned it to face the wall. Now she turned it round and faced her own plainness. But it was unbearable. She lifted a paperweight off the desk and flung it at the mirror, smashing her reflection into a million pieces. She fell to her knees, the shards of glass cutting her, and wailed at her broken life. Her life had been a sham, her husband a false idol.

It took her some time to recover enough to get up and go to the medicine cupboard in the kitchen. She took out her heart pills and squeezed the lid. It wouldn't open. In desperation she poked at the lid, trying to push down and twist, but all she succeeded in doing was spilling the pills onto the floor.

Margaret scrabbled around after them and then gave up. What was the point? She lay down and curled up into a ball to keep warm, her hot breath fleeing across the shabby floor as she vaguely recalled that she'd meant to put more money in the electricity meter.

Chapter 11

The night before Walter had dreamed that he and his mother had been shot with arrows. As they bled to death, Walter had shouted and pleaded with the person who shot at them. Then, just before he died, he realised that his pleas wouldn't solve anything and that they really should go to the doctor. An arrow through his heart and through his mother's; it reminded him of the picture of the Virgin Mary. She was the holiest woman in the history of mankind. Is that how he felt about his mother? Was he too devoted to her?

He had taken a photograph of his mother off the wall to preserve it. He had never been able to find any of his father and had often wondered about that. The bright patch on the wall where his mother's picture had been for years contrasted starkly with the dull, shabby wallpaper around it. At the age of seventy-five, it was time he grew up. He smiled at that thought.

He looked around his living room. It needed brightening up. He rolled up his sleeves and fetched a bucket of water from the kitchen. Ted sprang over and began to drink from it.

'Ted!' Walter chided him and chuckled.

Ted woofed mischievously.

Walter poured some cleaning fluid into the bucket and took a new cleaning cloth out of the packet.

'Now, Ted, settle down,' Walter said as he dipped the cloth in the bucket.

He couldn't help worrying about Margaret. He would give Rebecca time to come and take the desk and then he'd call round. He wasn't afraid of having a row with Rebecca – as they said in his favourite westerns, sometimes you had to shoot it out – but he didn't want to upset Margaret either.

With a little tinkle of his name tag Ted lay down under the table and put his head on his paws. He was whining quietly. Walter could usually guess what Ted wanted but this behaviour was puzzling. Maybe his arthritis was playing up.

'You're getting old like the rest of us. Is that what's wrong, boy? I'll take you out after I finish here. We don't want to be too early to Margaret's.'

He began to clean the front window in the living room. The window cleaner had done the outside, but it was the inside that needed cleared of its grime. As he worked, the room filled with the new winter light.

'Tiring work, but worth it,' he said to Ted.

Ted shook himself and moved to a spot where the new-found light seemed to bring added warmth.

* * *

Rebecca rang the bell. She had tried to open the door with her front door key but it was bolted from the inside. There wasn't a sound. Rebecca banged the door so hard that flakes of red paint fell off onto the icy step. She knew that Margaret was an early riser, so where was she? Perhaps Margaret was trying to swindle her out of her inheritance in some way. Maybe she'd been getting advice from someone else. Well, she couldn't dodge her forever. She'd be back the next day; then Margaret would know all about it.

* * *

Margaret was stirred by the sound of the doorbell ringing, but when she tried to get up she fell. How wonderful everything had been in her dream – all warm and cosy – but the memory of it was fading fast. Sitting on the floor, she peeled off her cardigan and undid her blouse. She really ought to get up and turn the heating off; it was a luxury she couldn't afford. She'd lie down for just a few minutes more; it had been a long, long time since she'd felt so ... relaxed. She wiped her mouth and lay down on the cold stained carpet and slipped away into silence.

In the darkness of her dreams her husband stood glowering over her, his arm raised, his hand clenched into a fist. She got to her feet and asked him who he was. He struck her.

She fell deeper.

* * *

Ted whined and scratched Margaret's front door. Walter was concerned – she had seemed so grateful that he had offered call. Maybe she was at her daughter's house. Or maybe she'd become sick and been taken to hospital. Or perhaps she'd just gone for a walk.

Then Walter looked at Ted who was still whining and scratching the door. Walter trusted Ted's instincts. There was someone in, that was for sure, and he felt a sudden surge of panic fill his being like the frost on the inside of the window. Why was there frost on the inside of the window? The entire house emanated coldness. Walter paced the gravel drive in front of the house. He wasn't sure what to do. He shouted through the letter box: 'Margaret? It's Walter. Are you okay?' He clutched his arm and took a deep breath. The pain was sharp but it passed.

He had to act. This was the first time he cursed his hatred of modern technology. If only he had a mobile phone! He went next door but it was deserted, its windows like blank sockets; a 'For sale' sign had taken root in the front garden. He tried the next house along.

'Hello! Help! Is there anyone there?' he shouted, but if there was anyone there, they didn't respond. He banged the door angrily with his stick.

Back out on the street, he looked up and down. No postman, no milkman – no one on the bloody planet!

His desperation grew as he returned to Margaret's front door. If Margaret was as foolish and forgetful as he was, she would have a key hidden somewhere outside. He pushed a plant pot next to the door with his foot. Nothing. He ran his fingers around the doorframe, nothing except a splinter from the frame that made him curse loudly. A tear of panic ran down his cheek. He banged the door one more time, then slumped down in front of it, and as he sat there, he locked eyes with a stone leprechaun, its mouth contorted by weathering and old age into a twisted smile. He pushed it to one side and there was a key, a much better treasure than a crock of gold.

He snatched it up and put it in the lock, but it wouldn't turn. The snib must be locked from the inside. And if it was snibbed on the inside that meant that someone was in. Oh Heaven help us!

Walter shoulder-charged the door and fell back in agony, but the door remained intact. He tried to stand up but could barely keep his balance. Think, man, think! Perhaps the key wasn't for the front door. What other door might it fit?

He opened the gate at the side of the house and ran round to the back, bumping into Margaret's black bin on the way. He fell to his knees in front of the back door and prayed as he put the key in the lock. It turned with a reassuring click. What a relief! He let himself in and was horrified to find that it was almost colder insider the house than it was outside. Ted was tugging hard on the lead.

'Margaret!' he called. He could see his breath in front of him as he walked gingerly from one room to the next. 'It's only me, Margaret – Walter.'

The house was as cold as death. Panic rose from his chest to his throat, making him choke as he called her name. Ted pulled himself free and bounded off through the house dragging his lead behind him. Walter could hear him padding around in as much of a panic as he was. Suddenly Ted barked.

'Where are you, boy?' Walter shouted. Ted gave another short sharp bark. It sounded as if it came from a room off the downstairs hallway. Then Ted started to whine. Walter made his way towards the noise. Inside the old-fashioned study, Walter came upon Margaret. She was curled up in a ball and blue with the cold. He knelt beside her, afraid to touch her, and tried to control his own breathing.

At first he thought she had been attacked because of the state of her clothing. She was only wearing a thin blouse and skirt; her cardigan and shoes were lying beside her, and the papers scattered all over the floor suggested the place had been ransacked. She was clutching a photograph.

He took off his coat and put it over her. She murmured something.

'Thank God! Thank God!' Walter said, hugging her to him. 'Don't worry. I'm here now. I'll get help.'

He left her only to find the phone in the hallway.

'Which emergency service please?' asked a young man.

'Ambulance please. My friend is freezing to death,' Walter said, the tears running down his cheeks.

Chapter 12

Once Margaret was in the safe hands of the medics and Walter had passed on what he knew about her next of kin, he took Ted home and then got to the hospital as fast as he could. A nurse had called Rebecca to tell her about Margaret's hypothermia and how Walter had found her. Rebecca had got the nurse to arrange a meeting with Walter in the hospital canteen; the nurse told him that she'd seemed quite agitated.

Walter didn't know what to expect. Would she be grateful that he had found her mother in the nick of time or upset at what had happened to her mother? He glanced at his watch; she was already thirty minutes late. He looked around him wondering how she would recognise him – how would the nurse have described him. Old?

The cash register chimed as another customer paid for his dinner. Visitors sat around in small groups eating slowly; some patients who could leave their beds had joined them, an array of walking sticks and hospital crutches leaning at odd angles against chairs and walls. Nurses and doctors in scrubs sat around the tables eating and drinking and laughing as only those who worked so closely with death could. Death always won; with the cuts that ravaged the Health Service the grim reaper was getting the upper hand. Walter had heard the horror stories of pensioners so neglected that they died of thirst. Their angels of mercy only existed in the next world. Walter was determined that that would not happen to his Margaret. No! He would be there for her.

The staff at the hospital had been very professional and he had been reassured that she was getting the best care available. Sometimes people wrote off the elderly, but Walter had made sure they knew how precious Margaret was to him.

As soon as Rebecca arrived Walter spotted her. Margaret had described her to a tee – mid forties, leopard-skin skirt, hoops for earrings, not a blond hair out of place.

He stood up and held her eyes. He nodded at her and she pushed her way rudely through the tables towards him. She sat down opposite him in a cloud of musk and glared at him.

'Can I get you a coffee?' Walter asked while he was still on his feet.

She was silent and her eyes narrowed. He felt like he was being scrutinised.

'No, I've had enough already,' she eventually said, frowning.

Her eyes were red-rimmed and Walter assumed she was upset about her mother.

But then Rebecca rounded on him, wanting to know who he was, how he knew Margaret and exactly what he was doing in *her* house.

He had no easy answers for her. He gripped his coffee cup and held it against his chest. How he wished he was in Helen's café with Margaret smiling gently at him from across the table and Ted outside with a sausage. He could understand that Rebecca might not like him replacing her father in Margaret's affections, but the ferocity of her reaction when she heard the full story shocked him to the core.

'I'm her daughter. This is nothing but a flight of fancy. What are you? Some perverted old man she met on a bloody park bench?'

'Madam, I assure you our relationship …' Walter said.

'Relationship! Relationship – at your age?'

'My friendship – yes, my relationship – with your mother is entirely honourable.'

'Why the hell would anyone, even an old fart like you, be interested in … her?' Rebecca was shouting now. An Asian doctor who was sitting nearby glanced over. and the cashier scowled at them.

Walter didn't say anything. His mother, who would have described Rebecca as being in a 'tizzy', had always said it was better to wait until they'd calmed down. Still, he wasn't sure he could bear to hear another insult against Margaret.

'I know your game,' Rebecca went on, going red in the face. 'You're after my inheritance.'Suddenly it was clear to Walter why Margaret was so bowed and submissive. She'd had to put up with this. He stood up.

'Madam, I can appreciate that you're worried and in shock about what has happened to your mother, but I will not stand here and listen to these slurs on Margaret.'

Rebecca stood up too, seeming a little taken aback that he wasn't intimidated by her.

'I care about your mother a great deal,' Walter said, 'and it was only by God's grace that I visited her house when I did.' He didn't break eye contact with her. 'You can say what you like about me, but you will have me to deal with if you are offensive about Margaret. As my mother would have said, if you can't say anything nice then say nothing at all! So I'll take my leave.'

'So you think you're tough, do you?' Rebecca growled at him. 'We'll see who screws who! When I get my hands on Margaret …'

Walter banged his stick on the table. The canteen fell silent.

'Margaret, your *mother*, is in the High Dependency Unit, one step away from intensive care!' he said in a low, firm voice.

Then he turned and walked out of the canteen, leaving everyone staring after him in astonishment. He made his way back to the HDU's waiting room. He'd be damned if he was going to leave Margaret alone in this place when she needed him so badly.

* * *

When she'd first arrived, Margaret had been alert enough to see a male nurse enter the room and check her drip. She'd been in hospital several times before, but everything seemed alien, nightmarish. Then she began slipping away and coming back, in limbo between the past and present, between life and death.

* * *

'Who were you? Who are you? Margaret asked.

Her husband took a step closer. She could smell his breath. It reeked of brandy and abuse. She recoiled instinctively.

'You kept it all locked up in the desk. I could never give you what you wanted,' Margaret whispered. She could barely breathe.

Her husband, hovering over her, pointed to a family portrait that hung on the wall. It seemed to mock her. 'Thou shalt not … Thou shalt not,' her husband hissed.

'We're losing her,' she heard someone say.

She felt as if her spirit was withdrawing, retreating. Then the name that formed on her lips came as a shock to her and jolted her out of her resignation.

'Walter,' she croaked. 'Walter.'

When she awoke later she knew exactly where she was. She could hear hushed voices; people were standing around.

A nurse explained what had happened: she was in the High Dependency ward at the hospital. 'You're over the worst,' she reassured her and smiled.

Margaret tried to lift her head.

'Your husband was here,' said the kindly nurse.

'What!' said Margaret startled. She took a few deep breaths and her hands clutched the high metal bed frame.

'It's all right. Don't worry, he'll be back,' the nurse reassured her. 'He clearly loves you. He's only left your side to tend to his wee dog and pray in the hospital chapel. It must have helped. We were all really worried about you for a while.' The nurse smiled.

'Walter!' said Margaret, relaxing back into the pillow and releasing her grip on the bed, before drifting off to sleep.

Chapter 13

Monday 21st November

By 1.30pm, Walter was outside the Care of the Elderly building at the Ulster Hospital. He took the lift up to her ward and stood waiting outside the ward door until visiting time officially began. He held a box of chocolates; he couldn't think of what to bring that would express his true feelings. A patient wheeled past with a drip. The rain rattled against the windows above his head.

It was a week since he had found Margaret; he had been there every day. He only returned home to tend to Ted and perform his own ablutions. Rebecca had left specific instructions that Walter was to be given no information, but he had heard snatches from the doctors and nurses who cared for her, and one of the nice nurses made sure he was kept up to date. Indeed, Rebecca had gone so far as to demand that he quit his hospital vigil. Walter told her that that was a matter for Margaret to decide, not her.

He kept watching the clock on the wall. People of all ages were coming and going in the elevator. An elderly man was wheeled through the door chanting, 'Nurse! Nurse! Nurse!' Walter hoped the man had someone in the world who cared for him and that Margaret wasn't feeling as helpless.

Two o'clock on the dot and he pushed open the door and got as far as the desk. A black nurse wearing a crumpled white uniform and a bright smile came close and whispered, 'I'm sorry, sir, but the family said no visitors.'

'I'll only be a moment,' Walter said, trying not to sound as desperate as he felt.

The nurse turned away from him. Walter tugged her white sleeve. 'I just want to see her for a moment.'

The nurse looked tired and not unsympathetic, but said, 'Sorry, but rules are rules.'

His shoulders slumped and his stick wearily clicked against the floor as he made his way back to the ward doors.

'Walter? Walter!' Her voice was faint but he recognised it at once.

'Margaret! Thank heavens!' Walter called back.

The nurse looked at him for a moment, then sighed and with a half smile, nodded. Walter made off in the direction of Margaret's voice as fast as he could, following the yellow line to her room.

Walter sat on the cheap plastic chair beside her bed and held her hand. Margaret began to sob.

'I'm sorry. I didn't mean to upset you. … I'll leave,' he said, standing up and setting the box of Thorntons on top of her bedside locker.

'No, don't ...' said Margaret, taking a deep breath and reaching out her hand towards him.

Walter sat down again and took her hand in his. Her arm still had a drip in it. He could tell she wanted to speak but seemed to be having trouble finding the right words. He was happy to wait.

Eventually she blurted out: 'My husband has another ... *family.*'

Walter placed his hand on his balding head. 'Come again?'

'I discovered where all our money went. He has another wife ... and family. Mr Brooks. At the same time that he was married to me!'

Walter was wide-eyed with astonishment. 'Are you sure?' he said, gripping her hand more tightly. So he was still young enough to be surprised by something!

'I read the papers in his desk. I might be old but I'm not doting.'

'Sweet heavens!' said Walter without thinking. 'Oh, I'm sorry – I don't usually blaspheme … What an awful discovery!' He couldn't begin to fathom the sense of betrayal she must be feeling. He stared out the window at the sky, trying to think of something to say or do that would make her feel better. A bird flew past, looking for shelter.

'My whole life … everything's been wrong … every thought … everything he did,' Margaret said.

Walter held his breath.

A cheerful young male orderly with bright white trainers and a squeaky trolley stuck his head round the door. 'Cannae get yuz a cuppa?'

Neither Walter nor Margaret answered him.

'Nae problem,' the orderly mumbled, and off he went, his trolley squeaking its way down the corridor.

The daily business of the ward faded into the background as Margaret started to cry again. 'Who knew? I'll have to tell her,' she said between sobs. 'I have to. I've no choice.'

Walter listened. Rebecca was coming at four o'clock. This was something Margaret had to do alone.

The black nurse appeared at the door. 'Oh dear, you're very upset, Margaret,' she said. 'I think it's time to end your visit with your friend. We can't have you getting stressed. Come on, sir. I think Margaret's had enough for today.'

Walter got up and walked to the door. 'I'll just be outside,' he said to Margaret. 'Not very far at all.'

'Ahhhh, here is Dr Summers,' said the nurse.

Walter would have mistaken the doctor for a child if he hadn't been wearing a stethoscope and white coat, and carrying a clipboard.

* * *

'You're through the worst now,' the doctor pronounced after feeling her pulse and checking her chart.

'I'm not through the worst yet,' Margaret replied. 'I'm nowhere near through the worst.'

Dr Summers shrugged. 'I know it's hard, but you've got to be strong. Medically, considering your age and the scare, you've done really well. You had us very worried.'

'When can I see Walter and Ted?' Margaret said. She was becoming confused. Sometimes she wasn't sure if she was awake, dreaming or dead. She wrapped Walter's name around her like swaddling and felt herself drift off into a restful sleep.

Once breakfast was over the next day, she was deemed 'out of trouble' and moved from the High Dependency ward to her own room on the Geriatric ward. The room had a tall window through which crisp winter sunlight streamed.

The orderlies and staff went about their business giving Margaret a sense of life, not death. But she felt oppressed by everything around her – the noise, the brightly coloured walls, all that daylight. Her lunch lay on the tray in front of her half eaten. They had doubled her portions to encourage her to eat more, but her appetite wasn't great and she needed to get her strength back. She had to be strong for Rebecca. Things had to be sorted.

Walter popped his head round the door. His coat was crumpled and he had dark rings around his eyes.

'I need you to get some papers from the house for me,' Margaret said. 'If you can excuse the mess.'

Walter placed a reassuring hand on her arm and nodded. 'Bring them here – photographs, bank statements, everything,' said Margaret handing him her house key.

'I'll be back as soon as I can,' said Walter.

* * *

Later, when Walter returned, Margaret put the documents he brought into the top drawer of her bedside cabinet. The label on the drawer read 'Medications Only'; now it contained something much more potent.

Walter sat quietly at the side of the bed. 'I hope your recovery is speedy. I've been so worried. I never knew I could feel this way about anyone.' He blushed.

An elderly lady with pinned-up hair wheeled her drip past the door.

Walter pulled his chair closer. 'I felt so ... so lost. The very thought of you not being around. I was ...'

Margaret squeezed his hand. 'I'm still here,' she said, smiling.

'So where do we go from here?' he asked. 'I don't want to lose you again.'

'Nor I you.'

'May I suggest that I'm here whenever your daughter arrives?'
She patted his hand. 'This is something I've got to do alone.'

Walter nodded, and began to chat to her about Ted and the
walks they'd had in the last few days.

Just as he was leaving Margaret to go and feed Ted, the doors
of the lift pinged open and Rebecca stepped out. She glared at him,
her lips forming a thin red slash across her face. Walter politely
tipped his hat and got into the lift; as the doors closed, he quietly
asked the Lord for one last favour.

* * *

Margaret asked the nurse if she would close the door. Rebecca
looked puzzled. Margaret opened the top drawer of her cabinet,
pulled out all the documents and photographs and handed them to
Rebecca.

Her daughter sat back on the plastic chair and scanned through
them. Taken together it formed the narrative of another family in
Loghran, a village just twenty miles away. There were their names,
their faces, the bank accounts; Rebecca pored over page after page,
frowning with concentration and not saying a word.

'I look more like them than I look like you,' she said eventually.
'Still ... as Freddie Mercury said, the show must go on.'

'You're wicked!' Margaret said in a low steady voice.

She rested her head against the pillow and looked at Rebecca.
She was surprised by daughter's self-control. It was the same
Rebecca: fashionable red dress tied round the waist with a cord that
wouldn't have looked out of place round a monk's habit; heavy
make-up. But there was something different about her face.
Margaret tried to work out what it might be. Was she annoyed that
her mother, the woman she considered to be a big burden, and to
whom she felt bound by ties of blood and flesh, was able to deliver
such a blow? Yet Margaret knew that in reality there were no ties,
no need to feel burdened.

But then the real Rebecca exploded. 'You're senile. I'll have you put away. Do you think I'm stupid? Do you think you can put me and my kids through this? You've made all this rubbish up just to con us out of our inheritance.'

'It's the truth,' Margaret said calmly.

Rebecca was too absorbed in her tirade to stop and listen. 'What exactly are these bits of paper supposed to prove?' She lifted one of the bank statements and tore it into pieces. They fluttered to the floor around her.

This was the Rebecca that Margaret was familiar with.

'There must be a hundred explanations for these,' Rebecca went on, stabbing at the pile of papers lying on the bed. She wiped away a tear and swallowed. 'I've spent time and money on you all these years and for what? … This is how you repay me? With lies and deceit like this?' Rebecca was shrieking now.

A nurse opened the door, her dark eyes showing concern. 'Is everything okay in here?' she asked.

It had begun to snow again, large white flakes hitting the window, demanding to come in, then melting. Rebecca sat in the chair and snivelled, her make-up streaking down her face.

The nurse became compassionate. 'There, there. I know it's shocking to see your mother in such distress. She was a very lucky lady. But she's going to be okay now,' she said, placing a reassuring hand on Rebecca's shoulder. 'I'll leave you for a moment. But you must try and settle.' The nurse nodded and disappeared.

Rebecca's sobs gradually tailed off. 'I've got to go to ... I've to take the twins to a birthday party,' she said eventually. 'Then I've to go to ...'

'I'm sorry. I'm really sorry,' Margaret said. She knew she had more to tell her but it could wait.

'You're always sorry. You've been sorry your whole life,' Rebecca said, picking at fluff on her dress.

'It's not my fault,' Margaret replied.

Rebecca turned on her. 'What did you say?' she hissed.

'It's not my fault,' Margaret repeated.

Rebecca's mouth fell open and she stared at Margaret goggle-eyed.

Margaret held her stare. 'There's something else I need to tell you. I've met somebody.'

'So that dirty old man really is having an affair with you!'

'He's not a dirty old man. He's a lovely kind gentleman. He's been there for me. He's come every day to visit me here. He cares about me.'

'You're a withered old hag,' Rebecca said, her mouth barely opening. 'You're like a rotten, old, shrivelled apple. Who's going to care about you?'

Margaret sat up. 'He's my friend. In fact, we're more than friends.'

Rebecca jumped up and raised her arm. 'It's a betrayal. What about my father? What about his memory? You're evil. And at your age too. What about me and the kids? I don't believe this is happening to me. You're mad! That's what it is, you've gone senile! I told people I thought you might have dementia but I didn't believe it until now. I'm going to have you put you in a home ...' She began to cry again. 'You're just doing it to get attention. That's what it is. But if you think I'm going to let your fancy man get his hands on my inheritance you've another thing coming.' Rebecca appeared to be more bewildered than angry; never had she looked more like Mr Brooks.

Margaret reached for the emergency cord but a stern-faced nurse came in just before she pulled it.

'I think it would be better if you left now and went home,' the nurse said to Rebecca. 'You look very upset and I can't have you upsetting my patient.'

She took Rebecca gently by the arm and escorted her out, Rebecca stomping sulkily towards the lift.

* * *

Rebecca cut through Accident and Emergency to get to the main door of the hospital. She could see many people with physical wounds – cut heads, arms in slings, bloodied fingers – and she couldn't help wishing she had a wound that everyone could see, something that would take her mind off her inner pain. She pulled herself up a little straighter as she walked out into the cold air towards her jeep.

She'd left the twins inside it. They were drawing pictures in the condensation on the windows. They looked like primitive cave drawings, Rebecca thought.

'Mummy, why is your face all wet?' Michael asked as soon as she got in.

'You said you were only going to be ten minutes but you've been aaagggges,' whined Martin.

Michael banged his toy helicopter against the window. 'Yeah, you're a liar.'

'Li-ar, li-ar, pants on fi-re,' shouted Martin giggling.

Rebecca turned the key in the ignition and slipped into first gear.

'Li-ar, li-ar, pants on fi-re. Li-ar, li-ar, pants on fi-re,' chanted Michael and Martin together.

Rebecca drove to the barrier and put her parking ticket in the machine.

'Will you two little pricks pipe down!' she yelled. 'I need to make an important call – one I should have made years ago,' she mumbled, pulling over and getting out her phone.

Chapter 14

The café seemed just the same as it always was – tea-coloured walls, chequered tablecloths, little pots of sugar sachets on the tables. 'Love Me Do' was playing on the radio in the background. But something was different. As soon as Helen saw Walter and Margaret smile at each other she knew something had changed.

Walter pointed to the large mock train station clock that ticked above the counter. 'Do you notice anything about the clock?'

Margaret looked at it before returning her gaze to Walter. 'It's supposed to be old but it's actually very new?' she suggested.

Walter nodded. 'It's going slowly, and for us at our age, that's nothing short of a miracle.'

Helen, her cheeks flushed, wiped her hands on her apron and busied herself about the counter, trying not to let them see that she was listening.

Margaret gave Walter a bright open smile. 'I've lost everything I thought important,' she said, 'and now that I've got used to it, it doesn't feel so bad.'

Walter reached his hand out through the cups and plates until it met hers in the middle.

'I never thought ...' Margaret couldn't finish her sentence. She was grinning like a schoolgirl.

Walter didn't withdraw his hand; The Beatles song came to an end with a final 'You know I love you.'

'Everything has changed,' she said. 'I feel like I've been a fool all my life – the way my mother once told me about. She was ...'

The door opened with a jangle as Joe came in, stomping snow off his boots. Honestly, workmen and their double time! thought Helen. He nodded at her, sat down at his usual table by the door and began reading *The Sun*. Helen went over immediately, clutching her order pad to her chest.

Margaret and Walter had lowered their voices; Helen strained to hear what they said. Her mother used to say that Helen could hear the grass grow. Helen took Joe's order for an Ulster fry.

Margaret said something that was clearly important – she'd leaned forward in her chair and squeezed Walter's hand.

'One fried egg?' Helen asked Joe while trying to read Walter's lips.

'No, two,' Joe replied.

'No sausages?'

'Two sausages!' Joe said impatiently, tapping his dirty yellow hard hat that sat on the table.

Helen could resist no longer. She wandered over to Walter and Margaret's table and collected their empty plates. Joe sighed and went back to reading *The Sun*.

'Don't you two duckies look nice together?' Helen said.

Walter and Margaret smiled at each other and didn't blush.

'Could we have …' Walter began.

'… two more cups of Auntie Helen's special brew?' Helen said, chuckling. 'That'll soon knock the cold outta the pair of ya.'

Margaret and Walter looked at each other and started to laugh.

'We're too old to have aunties!' Margaret said.

Ted was on his back, paws pointing to the ceiling and wriggling around with delight after eating one of Helen's sausages. Helen stopped to tickle his tummy. He wagged his tail and stood up, giving himself a good shake.

'You're never too old to have aunties,' said Helen and winked at them. 'The tea's on me!'

She went off behind the counter with their empty mugs. Ted yawned lazily, stretched and lay down at Margaret's feet. Helen returned with the refilled mugs and hovered nearby after she'd set them down on the table. Margaret and Walter stopped talking and looked at her.

'Well … just shout if you need anything,' she said, eventually taking the hint, and went back behind the counter.

She tried to make Joe's fry while keeping an eye on the old couple.

* * *

Margaret passed Walter a photograph; it showed Mr Brooks and his 'other' wife holding hands. Mr Brooks was smiling in the photograph. Walter looked at it but remained silent.

'He'd never liked the word "husband",' Margaret said. 'Now I think I know why. It probably pricked his conscience. What a hypocrite. I remember him going to Bible study. And I remember the contempt he treated me with.'

'You use the word "remember" a lot. I know memories are sometimes all people of our age have, but it need not always be the case. We can make new memories of our own,' Walter said.

'Yes, you're right, Walter … and I'm feeling better on the outside. Really. But I need to know who she was and if they had children.'

Walter frowned. 'Margaret, might I suggest that that might not be very helpful? It's not what has happened in the past that's important now, it's what can happen in the future. It's the future that's important … There I've said it.'

'The future?'

'While I prayed in the hospital church I came to realise just what was most important.'

Margaret rubbed the lobe of one ear, a frown on her face. 'I need to lay a ghost to rest before I go thinking about the future.'

'I've had my share of … ghosts. I heard a song on the radio not long ago. I think I was here at the time. It went something like 'You've got stuck in a moment and you can't get out of it', and I knew that was me. Before I met you, I thought being alive meant just breathing. But being alive is so much more than that.'

Margaret wrung her hands at Walter's little speech. 'But I need to know the truth. I deserve to know the truth about my past.'

'I'm worried that that might not be the best course of action. But it goes without saying that I'll support you, whatever you do.' Walter rubbed his left arm absent-mindedly.

Margaret nodded and smiled warmly. 'Thank you. That means a great deal. You're so unlike anybody I've ever met.'

Ted whined quietly, stood up and stretched out his front paws, his bottom in the air. He gave a little yelp. The cold was probably affecting his arthritis, Walter thought.

'It's time to go and find out the truth,' Margaret said.

Walter nodded. He looked at the clock as they left the warm café and for the first time wondered what tomorrow would bring. Margaret was right – it was time for the truth.

They took a bus to the city centre, but the weather turned against them as they walked the freezing half mile out the other side of the city to arrive a grand mock Tudor house. Walter had offered to pay for a taxi but Margaret said she needed to walk, and Ted didn't seem to mind either. Walter knew the saying, that every long journey began with one step, but in this weather, he thought that was taking it a bit far.

'They may not live here anymore,' Walter said, staring up at the place.

'They still live here,' said Margaret with confidence. Ted pawed her foot; he seemed anxious to continue his walk.

'What will you say?' Walter asked, more as a way of preparing Margaret for what might happen next.

'I don't know yet, but I've got to see.'

'It's cold,' said Walter, 'and you're only getting over your hypothermia.'

'I want to ... I want to know,' Margaret insisted.

Walter wondered how such a perceptive woman could not see the mistake she was making. Then he realised that he clung on to his dead mother, even though she was long gone. What right had he to stop Margaret finding out the truth about her past?

Walter guessed this other woman didn't need to worry about buses or cold walks. A brand new silver BMW sat lazily in the drive; the house itself was immaculately maintained. Walter wondered if Margaret was comparing it to her own run-down house and her relative poverty. What betrayal!

Margaret put her hands in her shabby coat pocket and took out two photographs, one of her own wedding and one of the other woman's, with Mr Brooks playing the part of groom in both. Ted whined and pulled his ears back. Margaret turned to look at Walter. He grimaced and tried to smile. He wanted to go with her to the front door but she needed to make the last bit of the journey alone. Margaret opened one of the large wrought iron gates and began the long walk to the front door.

* * *

The wreath on the door proclaimed goodwill to all men. Margaret pressed the doorbell and it reverberated imperiously inside. A few seconds later the door was opened by a boy who looked to be a few years younger than the twins. He eyed her up suspiciously.

Margaret was taken aback. She recognised him instantly. He had his grandfather's nose, his eyes and his smile, the smile she'd only seen Mr Brooks wear in his wedding photo to Grainne, the woman she'd come to visit.

'Hello. Who are you?' the boy asked.

'Is your grandmother in?'

'Granny!' he yelled into the house, 'some other granny is at the door.'

Margaret remained steadfast. Seconds later, a woman stood at the door. She was neat and well-polished, and younger than Margaret. The woman's clothes were bright and friendly; Margaret couldn't help but think of her own dull clothing. A little girl appeared at the woman's side. She had long auburn hair, a bit like Rebecca's, and she pressed her elf-like features into the fabric of her granny's dress.

Margaret looked at the children and back at the woman. Puzzled, they all stared back at Margaret. Then Margaret nodded politely to Grainne, a simple gesture of acknowledgement.

'I'm sorry,' Grainne said. 'We have no money for charity.'

A seagull cawed overhead and flew inland, a sign there were storms ahead. Without saying anything, Margaret turned and walked back to join Walter at the gate. Silently, Walter put his arm around her.

'Who was that, Granny?' the little girl lisped.

'Yeah, what does that funny woman want?' the boy asked.

'No idea. Whatever it was she didn't get. Now, who's for Sugar Puffs?'

'Me!' chimed the children as the woman closed the front door.

The word 'me' echoed along the drive to Margaret and Walter standing at the gate. Margaret let go of the photographs in her pocket and took Walter's arm as they walked away down the road back to the city centre.

* * *

Rebecca held the phone tight to her ear. Her voice was low, a technique she'd learned to use to help her hide the emotion in her voice.

'I'm phoning to talk to you about money. The kids and I are doing great without you. … Why are you laughing? The divorce is coming through and you won't get a penny.'

Blake's girlfriend came on the phone, her voice sultry and posh. 'I must say, Blake and I find your greed refreshing.'

Rebecca listened to their mock fight for the phone. There was suppressed sniggering.

'Have you been drinking?' Blake said, having obviously regained control.

'No, I have not been drinking,' Rebecca snapped. 'But it sounds like you have!'

'We like to have a nice red at the weekends, but we drink responsibly – unlike you.' Rebecca could hear the sneer in his voice.

'Drink or no drink, I'm still the woman you love … or loved,' Rebecca yelled down the phone, hoping the other woman could hear. 'You think you're so perfect. Will I tell *her* some of the things you get up to? Maybe I should tell her about how you used to hit me and spank the kids. You were the big man then!'

'I'm putting the phone down now,' snapped Blake.

'Wait! … Margaret's become senile,' Rebecca said quickly.

'So what? I left because of you, Rebecca. It had nothing to do with Margaret. There was no room in your life for anything but those twins, and they're little monsters.'

'How dare you! They're your children too. And they miss you. Don't hang up. I've something to tell you.'

Blake sighed. 'You've twenty seconds.'

'I didn't have enough money. That's why you really left us, isn't it? Well, Margaret's gone senile and I'm putting her into a home.'

'I'll believe that when I see it. The old bitch will outlive us all, and dynamite won't get her out of that house.'

'Can we meet?'

'Okay, we can meet, but this better not be one of your fantasies.'

'Oh, brilliant. Thank you. We can discuss money and … our other
    issues. There was silence at the other end. 'Say something,'
Rebecca begged.

'I don't want to end up talking about old times. Where and when do you want to meet?'

Rebecca could imagine the looks that Blake and his girlfriend were exchanging at the other end of the phone, but she felt comforted knowing that soon she'd be able to put Margaret in her place and get what was rightly hers at last.

* * *

Margaret scrubbed at the mark left on the wall where the clock had once been; the dark outline had almost disappeared. Looking around she realised the whole room was full of dark patches from possessions Rebecca had taken. The gloomy shape of the study desk would leave the darkest mark of all; its legs had weighed heavily on the carpet, leaving an indelible imprint.

She picked up a brown blanket from the sofa and threw it over the desk. There! She didn't have to look at it anymore. The desk had spewed what was left of its contents onto the floor. She wondered if it contained any more pain. She didn't feel up to going through the rest of the documents right now, but she'd do it soon. Rebecca was welcome to the desk; it no longer held any value for her.

Margaret looked at the house with fresh eyes. She wondered how much decorators would cost. She couldn't remember how long it had been since the house was last decorated. It would be nice to give it a fresh coat of paint, maybe buy some new rugs. For the first time she could remember, she was making decisions for herself and plans for the future.

Chapter 15

Christmas Day

Margaret held an orange in her hand. She closed her eyes, held it to her nose and inhaled deeply. She imagined the sun that blessed it and the hands that had plucked it from a tree. As she peeled it, she remembered eating an orange while she'd sat in her father's lap; she also used to get an orange in her Christmas stocking. When she'd removed all the peel, she put a segment of fruit in her mouth and relished the sweet tangy taste.

It made her think about places like Spain and she wondered what it would be like to walk through an orange grove. She opened her eyes and the first thing she saw was a glossy SAGA calendar offering cheap holidays abroad. She'd never even owned a passport. She was still staring at the calendar when the doorbell rang.

* * *

Walter waited on the doorstep until Margaret appeared. He knew she wasn't expecting him.

'I wanted to give you this,' he said when she opened the door. He handed her a small wrapped gift. 'It's long overdue, but I hope you like it.'

'I can't accept anything more. You've been too generous already. And anyway, I haven't had the chance to get you anything.'

Walter, who was in the process of turning away, stopped and laughed. He put a handkerchief over his mouth to stop a cough. 'Oh, don't worry about that!'

'Well you can at least come in, now that you're here!' said Margaret, holding the door open.

Walter and Ted came in. Walter noticed there were a few strands of tinsel draped around the place, but no other decorations.

'Don't you look handsome, Ted?' Margaret said, bending down to pat him. He had on a new collar and lead. 'Oh, you'll be the toast of every she-doggy in town!' Ted wagged his tail and gave a quiet bark of agreement.

Margaret made them both some tea and Walter sat at the table with his mug. He couldn't help wondering if he was sitting in the seat where that hypocrite of a husband used to sit.

'The room seems to be brighter than the last time I was here. Maybe the days are lengthening.' Walter said.

'I cleaned the windows and wiped down the blinds,' Margaret said and she disappeared back into the kitchen. She was carrying a tin when she returned. 'I keep these biscuits for the twins when they come. Thank God. Otherwise I'd have nothing to offer you with your tea! Take one. Take a couple.'

It was like an offering at Mass, and just as gratefully received. Walter took a chocolate biscuit; he'd worry about his blood sugar tomorrow.

'Light is good. Light kills old germs.' Walter tasted his tea. It was perfect. 'You make a lovely cup of tea!'

She offered him more biscuits. Walter smiled and took another chocolate one. 'Absolutely the last one,' he mumbled while he chewed. 'You're the hostess with the mostess.'

Margaret tried to smile but it didn't last long. 'Rebecca's going to spend Christmas with her *immediate* family.'

'Well, if you like, Ted and I will be *your* immediate family,' Walter said kindly, patting Margaret on the hand.

'You know, until a few weeks ago I'd never cried,' Margaret went on. 'But I think I've got it out of my system now. It hasn't been just about finding things, it's been about letting them go. But you're right about memories. And I'm grateful that Rebecca loves me.'

'Not only Rebecca,' Walter said.

His words hung in the air.

Margaret retreated to the kitchen to get a bowl for Ted. When she returned Ted wagged his tail as Margaret poured some milk for him.

Walter looked across the living room into the study. There wasn't much space in the living room and it still smelled musty despite Margaret's cleaning. The place was cluttered with old heavy furniture that was too big for the space it was in. Perhaps the cleaned windows and blinds would help shed new light on the old rooms.

Margaret seemed overwhelmed; she was pottering aimlessly from the living room to the kitchen. 'I'll bring the teapot to warm your cup,' she shouted in.

Walter glanced at Ted who was still lapping his milk; Ted looked up and wagged his tail.

Margaret brought in the teapot and as she stooped to put it on the table, Walter turned towards her and their lips met.

Margaret blushed, drew away. 'I'll switch the telly on,' she said.

Walter nodded, his face warm. He hid behind his mug while Margaret fiddled with the television. X Factor was on and Margaret and Walter pretended to be interested. A sixteen-year-old dark-haired girl was standing in the centre of a huge stage looking terrified. This was an experience she hadn't had before, thought Walter. New experiences were hard and they probably got harder the older you were. Then, just as the girl began to sing 'It's a little bit funny, this feeling inside', everything seemed to fall into place for Walter. There and then he made a decision; never before had a decision felt so right.

Margaret and Walter watched with rapt attention as the girl finished singing and the judges and the audience sprang to their feet. The applause was deafening. It was all Margaret and Walter could do not to spring to their feet themselves and join in. The girl was a sensation! The sixteen-year-old nodded shyly.

'It's easy to have talent when you're that age,' Walter said sadly. 'I don't feel all that old. In my head nothing much has changed. I just feel a bit redundant. But somehow I've felt younger since I met you. I was going to say something clichéd like I feel like a young man again, but I don't. I never felt as hopeful when I was a young man as I do now.'

Margaret nodded and they held hands without thinking too hard about it. Margaret leaned in close to him.

'I thought no one would ever love me,' she said. 'I knew it was just me, that I was unlovable. I kept thinking, real people have happiness. The most I could hope for was not to be —'

' — in agony?' Walter suggested.

'And the only way to make sure of that was to give people something —'

' — or be of use to them.'

'But we're worth more than that!' Margaret exclaimed.

'We *are* worth more than that.'

'We are.' Margaret smiled.

Walter felt as if he was holding her heart in his hand. 'I could never talk about my feelings when mother was alive, and I was too afraid to keep a diary in case she read it. But I'll never be embarrassed about you.'

'Has there been any romance in your life?' Margaret asked, blushing. She held his hand tightly, her arthritic grip finding new strength.

'Margaret! A policeman wouldn't ask me that!'

Margaret laughed. 'Well? Have there been any girls?'

'Well, there was one ...'

Margaret smiled and nodded in encouragement.

'My mother didn't like her,' Walter went on. 'She said I needed someone more like her and this young lady didn't measure up.'

'Did she say that to the girl's face?!'

'No.' Walter smiled, somewhat embarrassed 'She never ... er …'

'She never met her!' Margaret was incredulous.

'I don't think any lady would have measured up.' Walter shrugged. 'I know you were a married lady with a child, but I'm surprised you didn't have a string of admirers before you met your husband.'

Margaret abruptly let go of his hand and topped up Walter's mug. 'I was told no one would ever want me and that I was lucky that Mr Brooks was willing to have me.'

Walter sipped his tea slowly, his brow furrowed. 'Those people …'

'My family loved me. They made sure I never did anything stupid. They even made sure I didn't pick my own clothes. The first coat I ever chose and bought for myself was the one I got when I was going to meet you for our first proper … meeting.'

Margaret lifted Walter's unopened gift off the table and turned it over in her hands. Walter knew she was dying to know what it was.

'Those people, whoever they were, were wrong,' said Walter. I'm quite sure you were an attractive and capable lady in your twenties. Now you're an attractive and capable lady in your seventies, and you don't look a day over fifty.'

'Och, go on with you!' Margaret blushed and smiled. 'And what was that word you used – capable?'

'Yes, Ms Margaret, that's exactly what you are – capable … and attractive.'

Ted had started to pant. He had finished his milk and the room had got very warm.

'I need cold water,' Walter said cryptically.

'Walter!'

'For the dog!'

Margaret fanned herself with an old newspaper that had been sitting on the table. 'Oh, yes, the dog. Of course! And I should open your present.'

She let go of his hand and carefully unwrapped the little box. When she lifted the lid she gasped.

'A friendship ring! It's so beautiful – so, so beautiful.' Margaret's face lit up; then a cloud passed over it. 'But what if Rebecca changes her mind and comes round and finds you and me with a ring?'

Ted scratched the door.

'Then you can tell her that it's now official!'

'What? That I have a fancy man, as Rebecca calls you?' She was smiling shyly.

'Yes! Well, more than that, if you'll have me,' Walter said, kneeling. 'Will you do me the honour? Will you marry me?' He took her hand and kissed it, then took the ring from her shaking hand slipped it onto her finger.

'Marriage? … I suppose that would make an honest woman of me. … I will, Walter. Oh yes please. I will. I will.' Suddenly she gasped. 'Wait! Oh my God … Oh my God.'

'What is it,' Walter was very alarmed. 'You haven't changed your mind already?'

'No, no …' she started to laugh. 'I don't know your second name! I'm marrying a man I've just met – I was going to say, I hardly know, but I know you better than I ever knew Mr Brooks. I will! I will! I will!' Tears were running down her cheeks as she kissed Walter chastely on the lips. 'You can get up now, Walter. I've said, yes!'

Walter grimaced. 'Unfortunately I can't, Margaret. I've been down here too long!'

They laughed and laughed. Ted barked and wagged his tail.

Margaret knelt down beside him and they embraced. Then they helped each other to stand up.

'You old fool,' she said. 'I'm marrying an old fool.' She smiled. 'I'd better go and get the turkey dinner ready,' she said, but moments later she returned. 'I'm not making a turkey dinner!'

'Why not?'

'I don't like turkey and I've just decided – I'm never eating one again!'

Walter laughed. 'Next time, we'll have dinner at my house and I'll make dinner for the three of us.'

'No one has cooked for me since I was a nipper!'

'Then prepare for your taste buds to be tickled! Listen, Ted and I had better go now,' Walter said sadly. 'He's getting hungry, and I only meant to pop round for a minute.'

He walked to the front door, holding Ted's lead in his hand. Margaret opened the door and he turned to kiss her good night. Margaret lips were unresponsive for a second and then she relaxed in perfect union with him. Their kiss lasted much more than a moment; and so they sealed their future.

Walter waved to her as he and Ted made off up the street, Ted straining on his lead. 'Until we meet again!' he called to her. 'Your family must not know our plans! We're star-crossed lovers whose love must remain secret!'

Margaret giggled. 'Romeo and Juliet were thirteen-years-old and that ended in tragedy,' she shouted back. 'You old fool,' she mumbled to herself as she closed the front door with a smile. 'I'm marrying an old fool!'

It had been the best Christmas ever.

Chapter 16

It was the new year and time for a good clear out – to throw off the old and bring in the new. Margaret had made a new year's resolution to stop thinking about her age. In the last few months she'd learned that her age was no basis on which to make decisions about the future; she felt less old than she did this time last year and she had plenty to look forward to.

But she had often felt lost among the jumble of sorting it all out. For most of her life she had done as she'd been told. Now, she collected the detritus of that life – the photographs, the memories that were supposed to mean something but didn't, the evidence of a life imposed on her – moving from one drawer to the next and making choices for herself about what *she wanted* to keep.

She had watched a TV show where an expelled member of a cult had had his clothes and possessions burned. Mr Brooks had stolen her life and now he needed to be exorcised. She had opened the blinds in the house, let in more light, yet the narrow sun still cast a shadow that fell like prison bars across her face. Her husband's desk loomed like a scary monster in the study. The last time it had nearly killed her; this time she was ready.

She filled a bin bag full of his stuff – bibles, letters to his other woman, contracts, statements, lists and other useless things that had nothing to do with her – and dragged it towards the back door. It was as heavy as a body. The weight of the world in one bag. She quite fancied taking up a course of study – in English literature perhaps, or creative writing! She could buy as many Mills and Boons as she liked. Maybe she'd even read *Fifty Shades Of Grey*! She put her hand over mouth to stifle a giggle.

The doorbell chimed, intruding on her happy reverie. She immediately felt her courage seep away, but then something like defiance rose within her. She dropped the bag where it was and answered the door.

Rebecca marched straight in and stopped in the hallway. 'I won't be long,' she said, pulling a sheaf of paper out of her bag. 'I'll explain all this' – she waved the documents in the air – 'when I've time. I've made it as easy for you as possible.'

Her eyes fell on the bin bag lying on the floor behind Margaret. She looked back at Margaret, pushed past her into the living room and set the papers, together with a pen, on the table.

'Sign,' she said, switching on a smile. 'Sign there.' She pointed to the space.

Margaret had often blindly signed papers before. Now she groped around the table for her reading glasses.

'You don't need to read it,' Rebecca said. She picked up the pen and made a big X on the document, then handed the pen to Margaret.

Margaret felt the coldness of it in her hand. 'What is it?' The question came out before she'd even realised it.

Rebecca took a step backwards. 'What do you mean "what is it?" Don't you trust me?'

Margaret raised the pen as if to sign.

Rebecca sighed. 'Come on, hurry up. I haven't got all day.'

Margaret set the pen down without making a mark and clasped her hands tightly together, her knuckles white and defiant.

'I haven't time for this,' Rebecca said. 'Would you just sign the damn paper! The twins are waiting outside and I'm in a rush.' Rebecca, standing hand on hip, was wide-eyed, pale.

Without making eye contact Margaret shook her head.

Rebecca took a deep breath picked up the pen, clutching it like a dagger. 'Look, there's nothing to worry about. This is just to make sure that you're protected and safe.'

Margaret swallowed hard, hearing the words that she had dreaded since her excuse for a husband died.

'This'll make sure that if you have to leave this house you'll be looked after. The one thing that everyone agrees is that you can't look after yourself. The social worker needed little convincing after your last little stunt.' Rebecca was watching Margaret's face carefully. 'If you won't do it for yourself, do it for the kids,' she went on. 'They'll benefit enormously from the sale of the house, and you'll be around to see them enjoy it. What's the point of making them wait until after you're dead.'

When Margaret still didn't move Rebecca began to pace the floor. 'Sure look at the state of the place. It's a health hazard. Sign everything over to me before this other family decide they're entitled to a share. All you need do is sign.' She pointed again at the document.

But Margaret wasn't the pushover she used to be. 'I want to talk this over with Walter,' she said.

Rebecca licked her lips. 'Look, I'm sorry I spoke to you so harshly. But surely your family comes before that old gold-digger.' She walked into the kitchen. Flakes of snow were sticking to the window.

'Walter ...'

'I won't hear his name again!' Rebecca shouted while somehow retaining her smile. She took another deep breath and said more calmly, 'What about if I make us a nice cup of tea. You're probably exhausted with all this tidying up. Who knows how it's affected your mind.'

'There's no need,' Margaret said. 'I've never felt better. I feel young again.'

Rebecca's smile turned to a sneer. 'I don't care. I want the house.'

'I'm leaving everything to Walter and Ted.'

'Who the hell's Ted?' Rebecca asked quietly. Margaret recognised it as the calm before the storm and braced herself.

'Walter's dog.'

'A dog? ... A bloody dog!' Rebecca screeched. 'I've waited all these years for my inheritance and you're leaving it all to some dirty old man and his flea-ridden mutt?!' She kicked the kitchen door; it bounced back off the wall and smacked Rebecca on the shoulder. But she was impervious to any pain. 'That man has turned you against your own family!'

Silence.

'You've not heard the last of this!' Rebecca jabbed her with her finger.

'We love each other!'

Suddenly Rebecca grabbed the collar of Margaret's cardigan. Margaret looked her straight in the eyes without flinching. They stood like that for a few seconds; then Rebecca let go and stepped back as if Margaret had slapped her. She ran off towards the front door, tears streaming down her face and slammed the door behind her.

As soon as Rebecca was gone, Margaret expected to feel terrible – to regret causing Rebecca so much distress – but within minutes she realised she wasn't one bit sorry. She went back into the living room and tore the document into a million little pieces and threw them into the air, letting them rain down on her like confetti. She ran to the window.

'The cash point is closed!' she yelled as she watched Rebecca make a hasty three-point-turn in her driveway.

* * *

That evening, Margaret peeped out the window. The lights from the street lamps were shrouded in fog and looked to her like little halos. She'd never noticed before. She was noticing a lot of new things now. Yet in some ways, life had been simpler, easier, when she couldn't see clearly. Still, there was no going back now, even if she wanted to.

Suddenly she spotted something familiar out the window – a distinctive silhouette. It was them. As they got closer Walter waved. Margaret went to the door to greet her visitors.

'Well, how did it go today, my dear?' Walter had asked the question before he'd even taken off his coat.

He sat down on *his* chair and Ted lay at his feet, looking up expectantly at Margaret.

'She accused me of betraying her and the kids – of not putting family first.'

Walter was silent for a moment. 'You've done nothing wrong.'

Margaret looked at her feet. 'I know, but I feel I've done nothing right either.'

'You haven't betrayed anyone, except perhaps yourself. Here's real betrayal: this man I knew from work used to phone up his fancy woman in Wales and talk to her for hours on end. Then straight after, he'd phone up his wife to ask her what was for dinner. He was so lucky to have one lovely woman. I asked him how he could be so cold as to do that?'

'And what was his answer?'

'He didn't know.' Walter shrugged.

Margaret looked at the picture of Mr Brooks and decided to put it into the bin bag too. 'And what conclusion did *you* come to?'

Walter shook his head. 'That's it. I never came to one. Except that maybe love is fragile. It exists in the moment. That doesn't make it any less valuable though. What matters to me is this moment – this moment with you. I've waited my entire life for it. All of a sudden, all those silly songs make sense.'

Margaret stoked the side of his face. 'But I'm just me. Little old me.'

'That's the sweetest thing about you. You don't realise how special you are. If only you could see what I see!'

'Tell me what you see.'

'Someone perfect.'

'Walter! Your head is away!'

'If I could only find the words! You're beautiful. You mean more to me than any other person in my life – my mother, even Ted.'

Ted looked up at him reproachfully.

'Sorry Ted,' Walter said smiling. 'You look very pale, Margaret.'

She wrung her hands and looked at her knees. 'I'm not sure how to react. Compliments. I'm not used to them from anybody, especially men.'

'Get used to them, my dear. I plan to shower you with them.'

Ted pawed at his leg.

'You deserve compliments too, boy!' Ted rolled onto his back to allow his tummy to be tickled. Both Margaret and Walter obliged, laughing.

'Mr Brooks thought of me as a piece of his property in the same way as the desk was,' Margaret said. 'When I couldn't give him what he wanted, he lost interest. It was like someone switched off a light. The only value I had was the value he bestowed on me, and when he found me worthless … well, then it was all over.'

'There's this ballad my mother taught me. I can only remember bits of it. It was by Thomas Moore. I think it was called 'The Minstrel Boy'. It was about doomed patriotism and a kind of loyalty. It went something like this: "Land of Song! said the warrior bard, Tho' all the world betray thee, One sword at least thy rights shall guard, One faithful harp shall praise thee!".' Walter picked up Margaret's hand and pressed it against his cheek. 'Let me be your "one sword", your "one faithful harp".'

Margaret blushed and smiled.

'Imperfect and decrepit I might be,' Walter went on, 'but I'd sooner go to hell than say a word against you or run off with some woman from the circus.'

Margaret squeezed his hand. 'Before you get too carried away with your praise and your compliments there's something else I haven't told you yet. Something that might make you change your high opinion of me.'

Walter looked at her for a moment, then said, 'Well, how about a cup of tea first.'

'I'll go and put the kettle on.'

'Wait, I'll make it,' Walter said getting to his feet.

'God really knew what he was doing when he sent you here,' she said.

Walter went into the kitchen and returned shortly with the tea. He sat in the chair closest to Margaret and held her hand. 'Now, what did you have to tell me,' he asked gently.

'Rebecca isn't … Rebecca was adopted,' Margaret said in one breath.

Walter looked thoughtful. Then he asked, 'Does she know?'

Margaret shook her head. 'I never knew how to tell her. There never seemed to be a good time.'

'Now might be a good time,' Walter said, but when he saw the expression on Margaret's face he added, 'But we don't have to talk about this now.'

'Shall we switch the television on?' asked Margaret, relieved.

She pressed a button and the old black and white set spluttered into life. *It's a Wonderful Life* was on.

'This is my favourite film!' exclaimed Walter settling down to watch it, snuggled against Margaret and holding her hand.

'If my mother could see me now!' she said giggling. 'I'd always wanted to hold a boy's hand at the cinema.'

They kissed.

'Is your heart going to hold out?' Margaret whispered, tucking her arm under his.

'Who cares? You've got to die of something and there's no better way to go!' Walter said and kissed her on the end of her nose.

* * *

Walter left later that night. There had been a heavy fall of snow since he'd arrived and it crunched underfoot as he and Ted walked home.

A gang of kids went running past, kicking over bins and yelling. On any other night it would have made Walter feel nervous, but tonight nothing could disturb his inner tranquillity and sense of well-being. His mother had warned him about romance – that it just happened almost without you noticing, like that was a bad thing. She had been right – it did just happen, but it was a wonderful, joyous thing, something to cherish and treasure. The word that came to mind was 'eternal' – he would be hers for eternity.

One of the kids came running past again, face concealed by a hoodie and anxious to impress his lanky friends. He threw a snowball; it narrowly missed Ted's head. But somehow Walter knew it would miss, for tonight was enchanted. The boy ran off, laughing, to join his friends. Walter smiled. Someday, if the boy was lucky, he too would meet someone as wonderful as Margaret.

Chapter 17

Rebecca sat outside Margaret's house in her black jeep, a jeep that was two-thirds owned by the finance company. Thank God for mothers, she thought, or she wouldn't have the jeep at all. She glanced behind her.

The twins sat buckled up in the back, their hair beautifully cut, new designer Adidas Lights on their feet and wearing little grey suits with shirts and red ties. They were as neat as two dolls. Rebecca herself had gone to some trouble to look well-groomed and presentable. They looked as if they were all going to church.

'Mummy, who are those strange people sitting in that big car behind us?' Michael asked. 'Why are they watching?'

'They're here to help us set things straight with Margaret.'

'I don't like Adidas Lights anymore,' Martin said suddenly. 'I want Reeboks. Everyone has Reeboks.'

Rebecca held her hand up and waved. The driver in the car behind waved back. 'Now, I want you to be good for mummy. I'll be back in a minute.'

'Mummy, Martin's pulling faces at me.'

'But Michael started it … I'm bored! … When can I get my new Reeboks?'

'I want them first!'

Michael and Martin began to shove each other, their faces scowling in anger. But Rebecca wasn't irritated – she barely noticed them.

'Martin's pushing me,' Michael complained.

'Then push back,' was all she said, absent-mindedly staring out the window.

The boys stopped their squabbling, surprise etched on their faces.

Rebecca got out of the jeep and sauntered up to Margaret's weathered front door. She didn't knock but opened the door with her own key. She made a mental note to have the locks changed.

* * *

Margaret was sitting in her favourite chair reading the paper and she looked up when Rebecca came in. She was immediately on her guard when she saw Rebecca's red shoes and lipstick, her neat outfit and perfect make-up, like some savage prepared for war.

'Oh, I wasn't expecting you today … Shall I make us a cuppa?'

'That won't be necessary,' Rebecca said looking round, her eyes narrow slits. 'This place smells different … And you've been moving things too.'

'I thought the place would look better if it was freshened up a little.'

'As long as you didn't damage anything. The value of antiques can greatly be reduced if they're damaged.'

'That's not something for you to worry about,' Margaret said, looking down at her newspaper again.

'I'll be the judge of that … I've something to tell you.'

Margaret's unease intensified. Rebecca had clearly come here for a fight, so it was probably time for the truth. Rebecca deserved it, despite Mr Brooks's order to keep her adoption secret. Margaret stood up. She was wearing her pink fluffy slippers and still had rollers in her hair. Rebecca towered over her, but despite these seeming disadvantages Margaret was not intimidated.

'I've something to tell *you*,' said Margaret and pointed to a chair.

It was Rebecca's turn to look surprised. She sat down, knees together, hands on lap, and smoothed down her leopard-print dress.

'Two things,' Margaret said.

'Well, go ahead. I'm all ears,' said Rebecca.

Margaret wondered if this made things easier or more difficult. She looked out the window. 'It's snowing again. I'll have to get the path cleared,' she said.

'Get to the point.' Rebecca plucked a white hair off her dress and let it drop to the floor.

'Okay.' Margaret took a deep breath. 'Rebecca, you're my daughter in every way but one.'

Rebecca threw back her head and laughed. 'Just one?'

'I couldn't give Mr Brooks what he wanted.'

'And what was that?'

'A child.'

Rebecca shrugged. 'So?'

'Do you understand? I'm not your biological mother ... and Mr Brooks was not your father.'

'Is that all?'

'Do you understand what I'm telling you?'

'Frankly I'm relieved. Anyway, I already knew I was nothing to you – or should I say, that you're nothing to me.'

Margaret pulled away from her until she couldn't go back any further back. She didn't know what to do with her hands; they were shaking uncontrollably. Rebecca walked to the window, drew back a blind and waved. Then she went to the front door and opened it with a squeak.

'You've brought a social worker?' said Margaret incredulously. How had it come to this?

'No, not quite. That's for later.'

Margaret peered out into the hallway. There stood Mr Brooks's other woman, neat, polished, younger – much as Margaret remembered her from the last time they'd met. She led the twins into the house by the hand and let the door slam behind her for effect. She smirked as she walked past Margaret and embraced Rebecca. Rebecca dutifully kissed her cheek.

'Mum, this is Margaret,' Rebecca said gesturing towards Margaret with one hand.

'Gran, can we play with the birds in the cabinet?' Michael butted in.

'No, Mr Brooks collected them. They're not toys,' Margaret replied.

'Yes dear, of course you can,' said the other woman. 'They belonged to Granda Alfie and he'd have wanted you to enjoy them.' 'Thanks Gran,' they said running over to Mr Brooks's collection.

Margaret needed to sit down and quickly found the nearest chair.

Rebecca delivered the coup de grâce. 'Margaret, this is Grainne, my real mother. As you now know, your marriage to my father was a sham. We haven't been able to find a will, but we're quite sure he wouldn't have wanted you to have anything. So we're taking it all. Your best option is to co-operate and make things as easy as possible for yourself.'

'He was trapped into marrying you,' Grainne said, over-pronouncing each word as if she was talking to a child. Margaret could only see her lips move.

'You lied to me all my life. But I've known all along.' Rebecca sounded hurt but triumphant.

Margaret put her hands over her ears and closed her eyes.

'Now it's your life that's a lie, not mine! Isn't that right, Mum?' she said, looking at Grainne.

Margaret kept her hands over her ears. Only one sound came from her mouth. 'Why?' It came out like a wail.

'It was our families decision,' Grainne said. 'We loved each other and wanted to be together but he was twenty-eight and I was only sixteen. Those days things were different. Things had to be respectable. Alfie and I had a certain social standing to maintain. We couldn't think of just ourselves. We had to take our families into account. We sacrificed our happiness for theirs,' Grainne said.

Margaret swallowed hard. She felt sick.

'Alfie's father found out and took care of things,' Grainne went on, her plummy accent washing over Margaret. 'He was made to marry an available woman. You were available.'

Margaret could hear the smile in Grainne's voice. She couldn't help looking up.

Rebecca was sitting back in her chair now, one leg crossed over the other, one foot swinging idly. She looked impatient; this story was obviously familiar to her.

'I'd always wondered what it would be like to meet the woman that stood between *my husband* and me,' Grainne said. 'He spent every spare shilling on me but was forced to do his duty by you. He hated everything you tried to do – the housework, cooking, your servility.' She looked as if she was trying to convince herself.

Rebecca patted her hair. 'The bottom line is ... you're unworthy. That's why everything belongs to me and *my* family.'

'What kind of people are you?' Margaret asked. 'You ought to be ashamed!'

'There's just something in you that brings out the worst in us,' Rebecca said gleefully.

The bell chimed. Rebecca didn't seem surprised and got up straightaway to open the door. Margaret had shrunk into her chair as if she had been physically kicked; she felt as if she'd aged years in the space of a few minutes. It would have been better if she'd died months ago in the freezing cold house.

Suddenly Ted bounded in and sat in front of Margaret. His fur was spiked and he was growling. Michael tried to grab his tail, but Ted turned and snapped at him. Michael and Martin ran and hid behind their mother.

'I'll have that bloody dog put down,' Rebecca yelled.

Walter walked in to fetch Ted and then saw Margaret.

'Walter and Ted,' Margaret murmured, like a child with magic words that banished monsters.

Walter went straight over to her and held her hand. Ted barked and snarled at Rebecca, and danced around the floor as if he was about to spring at her. Walter looked up to see who else was there and recognised Brooks's other woman. He walked out to the open front door and stood beside it.

'Be off with you! … Now!' he ordered.

Rebecca and Grainne exchanged looks. The twins had started to bawl.

'We'll arrange a meeting to get this resolved. You're the mess on our shoes we can't get rid of,' Rebecca hissed. She grabbed the boys by the hand and marched out of the house. Grainne nodded and followed, keeping her demeanour as poised as she could under the circumstances.

Walter closed the door and rammed the bolt home behind them. He returned to Margaret and embraced her. He gently helped her over to the sofa.

'I'll get a doctor,' he said. 'My Margaret is going to be okay.'

'No need for a doctor,' she said. 'I just need a cuppa – and you and Ted. You're my heroes.' She bent down and patted Ted on the head. The dog looked for all the world like he was smiling.

'I'll get you some tea with lots of sugar for the shock.' Walter went into the kitchen, leaving Ted to look after Margaret until he returned. Then, in between the gulps of sorrow and tea, Margaret told Walter what she had just learned. She couldn't quite take it all in. Now she knew why Mr Brooks had always taken care of the paperwork and why the adoption procedure had seemed so quick. She'd been delighted with her daughter, of course, imagining that she'd found someone who needed her and would call her that most wonderful of things, Mother. But Rebecca had never called her anything but Margaret – she'd never been able to get her to call her Mum. So all along they'd been laughing at her behind her back. She'd been such a fool.

Ted jumped onto her lap and pressed his head against her chest.

Walter lowered his head as if in prayer. 'We can't change the past,' was all he said.

Chapter 18

Margaret and Walter waited in the café, their hands resting on each other's across the table top. It was their place, their safe place. Their tea had gone cold, but Helen seemed to sense that her cheerful attentiveness wasn't welcome today and she stayed behind her counter. Sitting in his usual seat was the workman, reading *The Sun* and waiting for his fry-up.

Their relations would soon arrive. The clock on the wall ticked like a bomb. Ted had been left outside in the cold, but sneaked inside at the first opportunity. He hid under Walter and Margaret's table, concealed by the chequered cloth, and kept their feet warm. Dread of the showdown that was about to happen weighed heavily in the air; it was high noon for Margaret, Walter and Ted.

Margaret had had a makeover: she'd had her hair done and had bought new, brightly coloured clothes. But Walter wondered how fragile this new confidence was and wished he could share it.

'I hate when things are so ... so ... up in the air,' said Margaret, looking into Walter's eyes.

'I do too,' Walter said. 'I do too. But even oldies like us can adjust.'

'You cheer me up, even ... even when I'm probably going to lose everything.' She held his hand tightly. Walter tried to imagine what she must be feeling. It was as if she was drawing strength from him. Eventually she said, 'Am I wrong to hope this will turn out okay?'

Walter struggled to answer and was saved by Margaret saying, 'I like that poem you told me about – 'The Minstrel Boy'. It's beautiful and kind of sad – about a place so near yet so far away, a place that had its own share of sorrows, about a battle between relatives.'

Walter patted her hand. 'I know it's old-fashioned to like poetry. And to think that something from so long ago can still mean so much now. I never thought that anyone else would understand why I like it so much. But you ... you do. It's significant.'

'I wonder how my battle will go.'

'I'll look out for you, Margaret. If they want to hurt you they'll have to get through Ted and me first. That's right, isn't it Ted?'

Walter felt the clandestine wag of Ted's tail under the table.

Margaret suddenly laughed. 'It's all so silly really. You couldn't make it up!'

'You two dearies want me to clear your cups away?' Helen asked from behind the counter. 'And maybe Ted would like a sausage.'

Ted poked his head out from under the table at the word 'sausage'. There was nothing wrong with his hearing!

'Yes, thank you,' said Margaret, reaching for her purse. Walter held on to her hand. 'Allow me the honour,' he said.

'When *he* was alive, every pound was a prisoner,' Margaret said.

'That part of your life is over. Those people who've made your life such a misery until now don't matter, and Ted and I will be with you to help you sort them out, once and for all.'

'Oh, I'm so glad I met you. I don't know what would have become of me otherwise.'

'You don't need to worry about that now.'

'But I'm afraid it's all going to go wrong ... between us, I mean,' Margaret said. 'I couldn't go back to that – to having nothing. If I hadn't met you I would just have existed – but I don't think that would be good enough now. Breathing isn't living.'

'It wouldn't be good enough for me either anymore. You're ... beautiful. Have I told you that lately?'

'Who looks at old women?'

'Old men.'

'You should have gone to Specsavers!' Age had not diminished the warmth of her smile.

Walter put on his glasses. 'Still beautiful,' he said, grinning back at her.

Margaret blushed.

Just then, Walter noticed them pulling up outside – three black cars, like a funeral cortege – and he grimaced. Margaret, noticing Walter's demeanour, tensed up but didn't turn round.

The bell on the café door jangled as Rebecca came in, carrying a takeaway coffee from the posh place up the road. She wiped off the snow on her boots and looked haughtily around. The workman looked up at her, his mouth agape while he squeezed ketchup over his chips, not seeming to notice how much he was putting on. Helen instinctively took up her position behind the counter, arms folded, almost daring Rebecca to say anything remotely disparaging about her café.

Rebecca's gaze finally settled on Walter and she stared at him for long moment. Walter didn't flinch. Margaret swallowed.

'What has this to do with your fancy man?' Rebecca said, pointing at Walter.

Walter tipped his cap and stood up. 'Won't you join me and my wife-to-be?'

Rebecca jolted at the word 'wife', but recovered within seconds, pretending to brush her skirt down and fix her bag over her shoulder.

'Let's keep this brief and painless,' she said. 'Just sign here' – she set a document down on the table in front of Margaret and pointed – 'and then I can get on with my life.' The document was bound in a fashionable folder, and looked as if it was long and complicated.

'I don't …' Walter began but Margaret interrupted.

'I don't have my reading glasses with me,' she said confidently. 'I suppose this is the deed you wanted me to sign earlier?'

'Sign!'

'I don't have a pen,' said Margaret.

Rebecca rooted around in her bag and produced a gold Parker with her name engraved on it.

'Ma'am, my solicitor will look this over and get back to you,' Walter broke in, half-standing and putting himself between Rebecca and Margaret.

Rebecca's eyes narrowed and her cheeks flushed. She scowled at Walter and pulled herself up straight, bringing her face very near to his. Walter was taken aback by such aggressive behaviour from such an otherwise attractive lady. Ted sensed it too from under the table and started to growl.

Rebecca hadn't seen the dog and jumped back in fear. 'I'll have that bloody dog put down. … This is none of your business. This is family business – and the family is all here.'

'Margaret and I are getting married. Ted and me' – Walter gestured towards the dog, half covered by the tablecloth – 'we're Margaret's family.'

Rebecca hesitated, but only for a moment. 'Do you think men really like you, you worthless old cow?' she said to Margaret. 'This crafty old bugger's only after the house.'

'I assure you, men most certainly do like your mother,' Walter said, taking a step to the right to block Rebecca's view of Margaret. 'In fact, this man loves your mother. I'm deeply honoured that she has accepted my proposal of marriage. I would've preferred us all to be friends, but I will not tolerate you insulting her. You must apologise immediately.'

Rebecca stamped her foot. Walter rolled his eyes.

'You're forcing me to do this,' Rebecca said, half turning to Margaret. 'Forcing me. I'm only being cruel to be kind.'

'Where are the twins?' Margaret asked.

The room fell silent. Even the workman looked like he might get involved; he had given up pretending to read his newspaper.

'Not far away,' Rebecca said. 'Everybody is here.' She waved her hand towards the window like a witch casting a spell.

Margaret reached round and tugged Walter's jacket. He sat down again. Ted looked from Rebecca to the café door, the hair along his back standing on end. The bell jangled, announcing the arrival of a tall, beefy man and Grainne, who had the twins in tow.

'Granny, look! Margaret and that other old man are here,' said Michael, tugging one of Grainne's hands.

Margaret stood up. 'Walter, let me introduce you. This is Rebecca's husband Blake, my two grandchildren Michael and Martin – and you've already encountered my husband's other wife Grainne,' she said quietly. She paused and then said more loudly, 'This is Walter, my husband-to-be.'

Blake thrust a fist towards Walter as if he was about to punch him, then opened his hand to shake Walter's. The man reeked of power and professionalism, from his gold cuff links to his shiny leather shoes.

'You won't mind if I don't shake your hand, sir,' said Walter, pointedly putting his hands in his coat pockets.

Unperturbed, Blake pointed to the table with his outstretched hand. 'Tea anyone?' he asked looking around at them all.

'We're all out of tea,' Helen announced from behind the counter. She was polishing a glass to within an inch of its life.

Blake snapped his fingers. 'Coffee then.'

'We're all out of coffee too.'

'Damn right,' the workman muttered, his cutlery rattling onto his plate.

Walter stood beside Margaret. 'We'll take our leave, Margaret,' he said placing a hand under her arm to help her to her feet. He could feel Margaret trembling, and gave her arm a little squeeze by way of reassurance.

Margaret stood up and looked straight at Rebecca. 'Why?' she asked.

'You're asking why I hate you? You're like an old woman in the market who sells fish. I was laughed at when I was a child. I didn't know how to do anything properly. And that whole make do and mend thing! Bloody hell! Why should I have to struggle? I want the best for myself and my children. I want a nice house, nice clothes, nice friends. You never gave me any of that.'

'Watch your language! Any more of that and I'll have to ask you to leave. You're disturbing the customers,' Helen said, nodding in agreement at her own comment. The workman nodded too.

'I'm tired of waiting, Becky,' Blake said, looking slightly bored. 'Just hurry up and get the old cow to sign.'

'Of course she'll sign, Blake. Just hold on.' Rebecca went over to Margaret and picked up the pen. 'Sign,' she ordered her.

'This is intolerable. Be off with the lot of you,' said Walter. He was losing patience. Ted growled in assent.

Blake glared at Walter, his small cold grey eyes menacing beneath dark bushy eyebrows. 'You'd want to control that animal. I'll have it put down. It's frightening the children.'

'You're doing that all by yourself, sir!' Walter said, clutching his stick tightly, ready to defend Ted too if he had to.

'You old ...' Blake growled. He turned to Rebecca. 'I hope I haven't come all this way to be disappointed, Becky … GET HER TO SIGN THE DAMN PAPER!' Then he pushed Walter, who lost his balance and fell back onto a chair.

Margaret gasped. 'Walter! Are you okay?'

Ted came right out from under the table, snapping at Blake and pushing him back against the door. The twins started to cry. Rebecca was shoving the pen in Margaret's face and screaming at her to sign.

'I'll protect you Margaret!' Walter wheezed, waving his stick in the air.

Suddenly the workman banged his fist on his table. 'They'll be no more of this!'

Everyone fell silent.

'This café is closed!' announced Helen, coming out from behind the counter and trying to shoo Rebecca and Grainne towards the door.

Blake fumbled for the door handle as the workman strode towards him. 'It's okay, I'm going … I'm going,' he said, waving his hands in front of him.

Helen, clutching a cold mug of tea, looked ready to throw it around Rebecca.

'I might have known you'd get it wrong, Becky!' Blake exclaimed as he wrenched the door of the café open. Flakes of snow gusted in. 'I don't want to hear from you or have anything to do with those little brats again!'

Rebecca followed Blake to the door in desperation. 'Wait, darling,' she called after him. 'Please don't go. I'll get her to sign … Blake.'

For the first time, Walter felt sorry for Rebecca.

'I've been misinformed about you,' Grainne said quietly to Margaret. 'I'll let the solicitors sort this out.'

Michael tugged at Grainne's dress: 'Granny! Granny!' But Grainne brushed his hand away as she left.

Margaret turned to Rebecca and locked eyes with her. 'I know I'm not your mother. But I'm me,' she said. She was flushed. 'I don't know what that means yet. But I do know I don't need you around.'

Rebecca's gaze dropped and she made her way towards the door.

'Wait,' Margaret said. 'You forgot this.' She bent over the document and signed it. 'You can keep the house and every stick of furniture in it, especially that stupid desk,' she said flatly. 'It was a prison to me and I don't want to be reminded of how I wasted my years. You can have everything. I don't care. I'll be living with Walter from now on.'

Walter smiled.

Rebecca took the document from her, checked the signature, then pressed the papers close to her chest. 'Thank you,' was all she said and she left.

It's over, thought Walter. Now Margaret and I can be together in peace.

Chapter 19

Sunday 22nd January

'The usual?' Helen asked, smiling.

Margaret and Walter nodded. They were sitting at *their* table, away from the draft at the door, holding hands. Ted looked in hopefully through the glass in the door.

After a few minutes, Helen returned with a pot of tea and two mugs and set them down on the table. But she didn't go far away. There was an air of expectation around the old couple today, a twinkle and a glint in their eyes, and she didn't want to miss anything.

'We have an announcement!' Walter said, not taking his eyes off Margaret.

Helen smiled at them and, raising her eyebrows, glanced over at the workman who had looked up from his newspaper. Margaret was blushing and focused on pouring milk into her tea.

'Tell Auntie Helen your news,' Helen said jovially. 'Have you another grandchild on the way?'

'No!' said Margaret emphatically. 'And thank God. Especially if they might be like the other two.'

Walter pointed at the chemist shop across the road. 'Does that chemist's sell circulation medication?'

'I'm sure it does,' Helen said puzzled.

'Medicine for colds and flu?'

'All kinds, I'd imagine.'

'Medicine for memory difficulties?'

Helen nodded and looked at Margaret, but Margaret was keeping her eyes on her tea.

'Do they sell wheelchairs and zimmers?' A smile was twitching at the corners of Walter's mouth.

Helen nodded again but frowned.

'Well, Margaret and I are getting married on Tuesday and we'd like to use the chemist's for our wedding list,' said Walter, beaming from ear to ear.

Helen put both hands on the table and laughed and laughed and laughed. The workman, Joe, had started to laugh too. Margaret smiled and held Walter's hand.

'I'm serious. And you're both invited,' Walter added.

Joe's eyes welled up. 'Wait till I tell the missus!' He came over to shake Walter's hand and kiss Margaret on the cheek.

'The tea is on the house,' Helen said loudly, giving Margaret's shoulders a squeeze. 'And I'm sure I can find some cake.'

'Well, I think that's a good start. A damned good start,' Walter said to Margaret. 'A thousand years it's taken to get here but it's been worth the wait. It's not the things that you do that you regret, it's the things you don't. We've not a minute to lose.'

PART 2

Chapter 20

January 2011

Until Diane came along, all beauty and brains, Joe's sole preoccupation had been building work. As one of the more insightful Christian Brothers at his school had observed, 'It's just as well you're good with your hands, Joseph Lonely, because you're no great intellectual.' He could still feel the childhood pain of the Christian Brothers telling him that God loved him while they knocked seven kinds of hell out of him for his academic failures.

Joe stood at the top of the scaffolding looking out over the building site below. He seemed to think more clearly when he was on a site, though he was sorry that he had to leave Diane. Without his work where would they be? It wasn't just about the money; he took pride in his work; it felt good to know that his hands were good for something.

Soon the scaffolding would be fleshed out with bricks and mortar and steel. It was the closest thing a man had to giving birth. His favourite movie *Bridge Over The River Kwai* captured something of his passion. Those men wanted to build something that would last, like the pyramids in Egypt, or Stormont Castle, or the city hall. Even council houses possessed something of that quality.

Joe admired the roof of the church he could see in the distance, glinting in the winter sunshine. One day, he thought, maybe I'll have the opportunity to build my masterpiece.

* * *

The priest was giving his address to the congregation. 'It is not the building that makes a church, it is the people,' he said as he examined the church roof.

Sunday was not Joe's favourite day. He hated being obliged to wear a suit, and the uncomfortable tightness of the shirt around his neck made the heat in the church hellishly unbearable. Joe looked up at the roof too.

'Don't come here on a windy day or you may get struck down,' the priest warned ominously. 'But it won't be God punishing you for your sins,' he went on, wagging his finger at the congregation, 'it'll be the tiles flying off the roof because it's in bad need of repair. These are bills, good people, that you're all going to have to pay.' He clasped his hands together in front of his chest.

Joe watched everyone around him. The entire congregation seemed to be taking this as their cue to read the bulletin. Only one lady, a certain lady whom he loved and who was sitting next to him, hung on the priest's every word, echoed his 'Amen' in her beautiful Scottish accent. Diane was looking particularly ravishing today, Joe thought. That flowery dress really suited her – showed off her curves and her shapely legs. He knew he shouldn't be thinking things like that in church. He noticed Diane's hand wander over to her handbag where she kept her purse; the priest would have no problem raising money for the repairs. Joe rolled his eyes and ran his finger around the inside of his stiff shirt collar. He looked around in the semi-darkness at the painted statues, the candles, the altar and glanced again at the woman beside him – the only reason he was here.

The priest had moved on from fundraising to his favourite topic – the true purpose of marriage: procreation. Every time he had been here, the priest always mentioned babies and mothers. Joe raised his eyes to heaven, or at least as far as the leaking church roof. He wasn't a particularly religious man, and couldn't fathom this idea that there was no point to a woman's life other than to be a mother, that she didn't have a role beyond motherhood. He thought he could see the cracks in the church roof – and in the sermon. None of the cracks would be sorted anytime soon.

'The Pope himself has a special devotion to the Virgin Mary,' the priest droned on. 'The story of the Bible is the story of Christ, and the story of Christ is the story of Mary, and there's no other way to tell this story.'

What was virginal motherhood, Joe wondered, not for the first time. He preferred Mass in Irish, mainly because he had no idea what was being said and he could think his own thoughts uninterrupted. His knowledge of the Bible was hazy, but his view of how it affected the young was not.

Diane turned, and as if sensing his restlessness, reassuringly stroked the stubble on his chin. He had forgotten to shave again and he saw her face break into a gentle smile that said 'I don't know where you'd be without me.' He didn't know either. Joe returned her smile, lowered his head and prayed for a child. They had been trying for so long.

As always, the Mass ended with the words 'Thanks be to God'; no one said those words with more sincerity than Joe. But Diane remained where she was, her eyes closed, continuing to pray. Joe knew why: she was praying for all the unborn children that they might be protected while the Virgin Mary, cradling the baby Jesus, looked on. He'd never liked the statue of the Virgin. He always thought she looked at him disdainfully.

Diane finished her prayer and looked up at him. He caught the distant look in her eyes, the one that said 'If only …' Joe smiled at her and tucked her hand under his arm as they stood up.

* * *

The end and the beginning had come at once. Or was it the other way round – the beginning and then the end. One day, their prayers were answered. Diane had phoned, like a modern-day angel Gabriel, bringing him the news that the test kit had turned blue: she was pregnant.

Later, they had gone together to the doctor's surgery, where their GP, an old man with a beard, told her to relax and not to get too stressed. He knew how much she wanted this child. He assured them the NHS would supply the best care possible. Joe believed him and Diane looked as if she did too. Diane earnestly shook the doctor's hand and opened the door.

'Mr Lonely,' the doctor said. 'A moment.'

'I'll see you in the car,' Joe told Diane.

She looked back nervously but Joe placed a hand on her shoulder. She flashed a smile at him that said, 'I trust you' and walked slowly away. Joe closed the door and sat back down on the stiff chair.

The doctor picked up the little white statue that sat on his desk; 'Hippocrates' it read along the base. He played with it in his hand before he looking up at Joe.

'Absolute rest and absence of stress are essential,' he had said. 'I'm a big fan of the poet Blake. In his poem 'Eternity', he said that you should kiss the joy as it flies.'

It was an odd comment, but Joe knew what he meant.

In school, the Brothers had talked about hanging on to things like happiness too much and then losing everything. So much was at stake that for the first time in his life he was truly frightened. He nodded his thanks to the doctor and joined Diane outside.

As husband and wife got into his car, Joe wondered if they would soon be getting out of it as a father and mother. He looked at the precious cargo in the passenger seat and began praying too. He remembered the last time he had been involved with doctors and nurses. He'd just lost his mother and was so distraught he almost drove into a ditch on the way back from the hospital. Please God, let this be the start, not the end, he prayed. If it could be the beginning, he promised he'd listen in Mass with the same gratitude his wife felt.

Chapter 21

Sunday 2nd October

Joe yawned, stretched and glanced at his watch. This café was simple but it suited him – it was away from the banging and clamour of the building site and it was cheap. He needed to watch every penny. Diane had resigned from her position at the fashion boutique. They had been sorry to see her go, but she felt it was her destiny to have this child and didn't want to do anything that might jeopardise its well-being. Everything she did now was in the baby's best interests.

Joe definitely needed to cut down on his spending at the pub. He never really felt comfortable in a pub and he hated the hangovers, but it was where his workmates hung out and he needed to show his face now and again. He didn't really get on with the new hard breed of workmen. The café gave him an hour's break away from them, especially the boss.

Helen, the jolly, busty woman who owned the place, grinned at him from behind the counter. He opened his newspaper and picked up reading where he'd left off.

The bell on the café door jangled and Joe looked up to see an elderly couple come in. Joe recognised the man, but he'd never seen the lady before.

'Walter!' Helen gushed. 'This is the first time you've brought your missus. You're a dark horse, you are. I thought it was just you and wee Ted!'

Joe rolled his eyes at Helen's foolishness. Surely she could detect the waves of embarrassment radiating from the old couple.

Helen flapped her chubby hands in the air. 'I'll make you both a nice hot cup of tea, and I'm sure I can find a sausage for Ted.'

Joe noticed the cute scruffy dog at the old man's feet.

The old lady looked dejected and sat down without making eye contact with anyone.

'Oh dear, Mrs Walter, you don't look too well. I'll put some sugar in your tea,' Helen said.

Joe was intrigued and positioned himself so he could peer over the top of his newspaper at them without being noticed.

'I'm afraid you've got the wrong idea, Helen. This lady and I are just acquaintances,' Walter said, half-standing.

Joe cringed and shifted a little in his seat.

'Mother of God, you can't fool me! I've run this café since my mother died nigh on twenty-five years ago and you make a beautiful couple.'

Joe had to distract Helen and stop her from humiliating the old couple. He got up to pay and emitted a rather large belch on his way to the counter. I'd rather be thought rude than do nothing, he reasoned.

'I'll be with you in a moment. These two customers are in dire need of a cuppa,' Helen said as she filled two large mugs with hot tea from a pot on the cooker and brought them over to the table.

'There ya go, lovebirds.'

'What am I doing here?' the old lady suddenly said. 'My Rebecca might call the house. She'll think I've abandoned them. And Mr Brooks's anniversary is next week. How can I ... Oh my! I'm going to have to go.' She quickly picked up her purse and stood up.

'Any chance of you taking for mine, love?' Joe asked. He was clutching a fiver – the exact amount – but he'd have been willing to pay every penny he had to stop Helen from sticking her foot in it again. Christ, even Kilwinner, his boss, was more sensitive.

But Helen was too caught up in the old folks' drama to take his money. Thankfully, though, she seemed to realise the extent of their discomfort.

Walter stood up. 'No, Madam. Please, finish your tea first ... or at least let me pay ...'

'I pay my own way!' the lady said firmly as she made her way to the till.

Joe banged his fiver down on the counter.

Walter opened his battered brown leather wallet and followed her. 'Let me at least pay for my own.'

The lady nodded, then took out her purse and set a pound coin on the counter. Walter set his own pound down beside it. Helen smiled at them as she slid the coins off the counter.

'Let me walk you home,' Walter said to his friend.

'Really sorry. I'm really sorry,' the old lady mumbled and with a jingle of the door she left.

'What's wrong with your friend? Was the tea okay?' Helen asked.

Walter shook his head and shrugged. Then he gave the dog a little tug on its lead and they both left.

Helen took the fiver from Joe without looking at him.

'The service is great in this café – when you can get it,' Joe said gruffly.

Helen playfully tried to slap his ear but Joe ducked her hand. He was too annoyed. He watched the old couple leave. For some reason, he felt as if he'd witnessed something very special.

Chapter 22

The following week, Joe was standing on the roof of a newly finished building looking down on the people below. An old lady with brightly coloured permed hair came out of the hairdresser's and rushed up the footpath with the enthusiasm of a teenager on a first date. He shook his head; what had she to be so enthusiastic about? After all, she was old! Then he realised that it was the intriguing old lady from Helen's café.

Further up the road, another woman got out of her jeep in front of a house and hauled a brace of boys by the hand round to the front door. Tut, tut, he thought, if they were my boys I'd be much gentler. Even from this height he could tell a lot about people's personalities by the way they moved, and this lady was a *strutter*.

Joe knew that their baby was going to be fine. They hadn't thought of any names yet – Diane didn't want to tempt fate – but if the Lord was kind and all went well, then life would no longer be the same for them. And whether it was the best child ever born or not but it would be *their* baby.

'You're beautiful, Billy,' Joe yelled to his best mate who was balancing precariously on ridge of the roof.

'Don't go all weird on me, Joe!' said Billy, wiping his face. He scratched his head. 'You've got issues.'

Joe grinned and merrily waved his hand.

The building shone in its completeness; Joe felt that biting sadness that always came when something ended. All that remained was the snagging list and then they'd be on to the next house on the estate.

Chapter 23

Friday 4th November

At the end of the working day Billy slapped Joe on the back.

'Easy!' Joe said. 'Are you looking for the soft spot for the knife?'

Billy guffawed. 'Come for a pint with the boys – to wet the bairn's head.'

'The baby isn't here yet!'

'Aye, but you've done your bit.' Billy grinned at him.

'Come on, Lonely, don't be antisocial,' Kilwinner the boss chipped in. 'Get your backside down to the pub for a pint.'

Reluctantly, Joe tagged along. He wasn't in the mood at all, but didn't feel he had much choice.

DB's was the cheapest pub in town, but it had a bad reputation for drugs and other illegal activities. It had no atmosphere – no easy banter between staff and punters, just a jukebox for music if the TV wasn't blaring in the corner. It was enough to drive you to drink, yet alcohol was not his drug.

Joe squeezed into a booth with Harry Kilwinner, his boss and one half of S & K Builders, the 'S' of the partnership having long ago disappeared. They were joined by five of the other workmen and the Governor, Kilwinner's henchman. Joe hadn't been afraid of any man other than his father until he'd met the Governor. He was a monster. It was rumoured that in the 90s, Kilwinner earned his money by hiring workmen to do a job, then walking around with the Governor after it was done saying, 'That's shoddy, and that's shoddy. I'm not paying for that … or that.' The workmen, under the shadow of the Governor, could only look glumly on and remain silent. It had been an employers' market back then; lots of men had been looking for work, and it had been easy to fire one batch and hire another. It seemed to be returning to that situation now. Worse still, no one was buying houses, let alone building them. The houses that they were working on had been commissioned during the boom; after 2008, the purchasers had been doing their best to get out of the contracts. Joe took little pleasure in anybody losing money, but what about the workmen? What about his job?

Billy sat beside him in the pub, cradling a pint of Nookie Brown, and staring at a short sitting on the table in front of him. Kilwinner was in his usual bullish form, holding court as he began his tirade against Northern Irish football players: 'Do you know what size feet Norman Whiteside had? Size fecking four.' He needed to be in charge and talking about local football was his way of wielding power over others. Joe, brought up in a Catholic household, had never watched much Northern Irish football. He wondered sometimes if Kilwinner did it deliberately to exclude him, but he knew deep down that his boss wasn't that smart.

In a booth in the corner two young people were arguing. Their conversation cut through the air; it was hard not to listen in.

'It's you who wants to make a big
scene.' 'Come on pay up,' she said.

'I'll give you a hundred a month.'

The girl was silent for a second, then in wounded voice said, 'Twenty-five pounds a week?'

Joe glanced up at them. They were so very young. The girl's eyes met his; Joe looked down and prayed that he'd never find himself in that situation. He should thank God that he was able to earn a living in a job he loved and wasn't young and vulnerable and adrift in a life with no prospects.

Joe finished off what was left in his glass and stood up to leave.

Kilwinner pointed at the stool. 'Sit down. You've only got here.' Then he turned to the waitress: 'Get him another pint!'

The waitress was very young – not much older than sixteen, Joe thought. She was boyish looking – skinny with pale pock-marked skin, short hair and a shy smile.

The Governor strode over to the toilet. 'If you hear a magnum go off it's me!'

'I take your glasses,' the waitress said in a heavy accent.

Kilwinner half stood. 'Polish! You're the ones taking our jobs!'

The waitress gave a little smile. 'Italy,' she said, reaching across the table for the empties.

Kilwinner grabbed her arm. The little colour in her cheeks drained away completely and she wriggled to escape his clutch. Joe banged his empty pint glass down on the wooden table and stared at Kilwinner. But Kilwinner only had eyes for his prey and he knew no one would get in his way. Billy held Joe down by his coat and tried to make a joke of it.

'Here, are you boy or girl?' Kilwinner said into the waitress's face.

'Girl.'

The bartender was paying attention now and came out from behind the counter. 'Come on now, leave Wiara alone!' he said.

Kilwinner, still gripping the girl's arm, slapped a twenty pound note down on the table.

The bartender picked up the twenty. 'What's your order?' he said as he retreated behind the counter.

'Another round for everyone,' Kilwinner said, tightening his grip on the girl. Then he added, 'Here, did you find her in the boot end of Italy?' He laughed raucously at his own joke. Billy chuckled along too, but Joe felt sick.

'Can I go now?' Wiara pleaded, looking at the spilled beer on the table.

'Well, what d'ya think?' Kilwinner asked his court.

'Let her go,' Joe said sharply.

The laughter stopped.

Kilwinner bent down and squinted into Joe's face. '*What* was that?'

'You heard.'

Billy gave a forced smile. 'Where's our drinks?'

Kilwinner released the girl, who went back behind the counter, but he continued to glare at Joe. 'You need to watch your manners, sonny.'

Joe shrugged and stared back. He was no frightened child. Kilwinner glanced around and spotted the Governor coming towards them.

'The big man here wants to point out the error of my ways,' Kilwinner said to the Governor, not taking his eyes off Joe.

Billy suddenly seemed to find the floor interesting.

Joe stood up to leave, but Kilwinner blocked his way and raised his fists in a mock fight. 'Big man gonna fight me?' The old man dodged backwards and forwards. 'Put 'em up! Put 'em up!' he said, making it seem like a joke. Only Joe knew it wasn't.

The Governor, like a well-trained dog, had closed in behind Joe and was breathing hotly on his neck.

Kilwinner grabbed Joe's arm. 'So, big man, what was it you were going to do?'

'I was leaving,' said Joe, and yanking his arm free, began to walk away. But he just couldn't help himself. He sighed, picked up what was left of Kilwinner's pint and threw it in his face.

Kilwinner staggered backwards, fell over a stool and landed on his backside on the floor. The beer stained the wooden floorboards like blood.

The others at the table pulled back into the booth, trying to get as far away from Joe and Kilwinner as they could get.

Then CRACK! Joe went flying through the air. He landed on the floor on his back. He rubbed his face and jaw where he'd been punched by the Governor.

The Governor bent over Kilwinner and hoisted him up with one arm.

'Get your hands off me, you overgrown ape,' a red-faced Kilwinner snapped.

The Governor let go of him and Kilwinner fell again.

'Jesus!' someone said and sniggered.

Kilwinner sat on the floor, the stains on his trousers looking as if he had peed himself.

The barman rushed over. 'Right, you lot. Out,' he said. 'You're barred. The lot of you.' He ushered Joe and Billy, then Kilwinner and the Governor out the door of the pub. 'And don't come back,' he yelled after them.

Once outside Joe slipped off without anyone noticing. He trudged towards the main road in the cold, his head aching from the beer as much as the punch.

Chapter 24

The next morning, Joe took his usual route into work, and despite driving more slowly to avoid the black ice and getting caught in heavy traffic, he was early. He stood outside the grey, damp site. It was almost two years to the day since he had started to work for S & K Builders.

He didn't regret chucking his pint over Kilwinner the night before, nor was he worried about any consequences. On building sites there was a fair bit of banter; one minute you'd be slagging each other off and bickering – there could even be a bit of the rough stuff – and the next you'd be talking like best mates. Joe did a fair job on site and that was what counted.

He went into the hut to fetch his protective gear, and shouted 'Right!' at Billy who was standing glumly outside having a fag. Just then, Joe felt a hand on his shoulder and he turned round.

'What do you think you're doing?' asked a cold-eyed Kilwinner.

'I'm putting on my gear and going to work.'

'I don't think you are. In fact, I'm bloody sure you're not.'

'What?'

'Put that stuff down and leave.' Kilwinner glanced behind him for reassurance; the Governor was standing, feet apart, shoulders squared, waiting to escort Joe off the premises.

Joe forced his hands into the pockets of his boiler suit. The sleet coming through the open door stung his eyes.

'You're no longer needed here, and since you've been here less than two years, I don't owe you a fiddlestick.'

Joe felt like planting his fist in Kilwinner's red smarmy face – his drinker's nose was an inviting target – and stepped towards him. But the Governor had been concealing a large spanner behind his back, which he now produced with a flourish.

'Never thought you were going to make it here anyway,' Kilwinner said, turning his back on him.

Joe looked from Kilwinner to the Governor and then walked out the door. He went back to his car. He couldn't have acted any other way the night before; his mother had always said he thought he was Harrison Ford, acting without thinking first, but that was just the way he was. He was glad to be seeing the back of Kilwinner and the Governor, but he'd miss Billy and the others.

Joe jumped into the car and drove around aimlessly for hours. His phone kept ringing and in a fit of anger he turned it off and shoved it in glove compartment. He needed time to figure out what he was going to tell Diane. He also needed to find another job – and soon. After all, they'd a baby on the way.

* * *

When he turned his phone on later he discovered that he'd missed it all. Diane had been calling to tell him she'd gone into labour, and then later the hospital called to say she'd had the baby, a healthy boy.

What kind of father was he that he couldn't even be at the hospital to see his son arrive into the world? What kind of man did that make him?

Excitedly, he turned the car round and headed straight for the hospital. The baby was something he had helped to create and had a hundred times more worth than any building he might have brought into existence.

* * *

'There's a problem,' the young Indian doctor told Joe when he arrived at the hospital.

'Jesus!' Joe exclaimed, instinctively reaching to push back his hard hat before realising that he wasn't wearing it. He realised that his scruffiness and his black eye from the night before were probably not conveying a very good impression.

The doctor raised his hand as if in benediction. 'Calm down. Calm down. You've a beautiful healthy baby boy. Eight pounds at birth. I believe the joke with such a large healthy baby is that it's already half-reared.'

Joe smiled. 'If you tell me that my wife is okay I'm going to snog you.'

The doctor looked a little uncomfortable at that idea and wobbled his head from side to side in what to Joe was a peculiarly Indian mannerism. But he was also smiling and the brilliance of his white teeth somehow reassured Joe.

'Please let me allay your fears,' the doctor went on in his sing-song accent, 'Physically your wife is fine. We can find nothing wrong.' He set down his clipboard. 'But she's refused to see the baby.'

'Refused?'

'Yes. I'm afraid so.'

'You must be getting my wife confused with someone else. Diane wanted nothing more than a baby! I've heard of birds and animals rejecting their young but never a human being.'

'It's not uncommon in humans. What we want you to do is bring the child to your wife and give him to her. Mrs Lonely and baby are both awake and alert, and now would be a good time.'

The doctor led Joe out of his office and through a communal area full of elderly people. Joe's shoes squealed on the shiny hospital floor as he entered the maternity ward. The out-of-date shabby furniture depressed him as soon as he walked in. 'Wash your hands', a poster screamed at him from the wall, and Joe, conscious of his building-site garb, scrubbed his hands as if he was a surgeon about to carry out an operation.

When he went into Diane's room he noticed the cot with the baby in it beside her bed. He tried to make eye contact with Diane but she just lay there staring at the ceiling, a shadow of her former self, as if the exertion of giving birth had drained her of all life.

The doctor was looking at the papers on his clipboard. 'Now, we have some formalities to take care of,' the doctor said cheerfully. 'Occupation of the father?'

Joe cleared his throat. 'Joiner,' he said. It was his turn to look at the ceiling.

The doctor smiled. 'You'd be surprised how many parents of newborns have no profession at all. Be glad you a job. Having a new baby is a very big expense. When a father can provide for his child he should be a happy man. The real tough guy is the man who gets up every morning and goes to work.'

Suddenly the baby cried out, its mouth wide open, as if disagreeing with the doctor.

Diane lifted down a set of earphones that dangled above her bed and inserted one in each ear. With a remote control she cranked the volume up and turned her face away from the cot. The nurse picked up the baby and tried to quiet him for a few moments before tenderly handing him to Joe.

He sat on a pink plastic chair and awkwardly cradled the child, worried his arms wouldn't be strong enough to hold the precious bundle. Overcome with emotion, he searched for the right words.

'Amazing,' Joe eventually said. 'Amazing!' He pressed the child gently to his chest and rocked him a little; the baby stopped crying.

'Now, why not pass Tom to his mother,' the nurse suggested. She slowly removed the earphones from Diane's ears and placed her hand on her shoulder. 'Look Diane, Tom's met his daddy.'

Joe brought Tom over to the bed and stood beside Diane, but she wouldn't look at them. He bent down, holding Tom out towards her. Diane didn't move. Joe could have understood any reaction, even hatred, but there was no way to fight indifference. His heart sank. He held Tom for another few moments and then returned him to the cot, full of pride and despair. Tom looked him in the eyes, his little fists pumping the air defiantly.

Joe sat on the bed and gathered his wife in his arms. It was like holding a corpse; she gave no response at all. What the hell am I going to do? he thought. He laid her back down on the bed, turned his back to her, and for the second time in thirty years, he wept.

* * *

Joe walked away from the hospital later that night, not bothering to collect his car from the car park or with a destination in mind. He took deep gulps of the cold air, hoping it would stop his nausea. What had happened to Diane? He couldn't believe how she was reacting to the baby. He battled his way out onto the main road, head dropped against the driving snow. Then through the blizzard he saw the glow of a neon sign advertising a happy hour in DB's, the pub they'd been thrown out of last night. For the first time in a long while, the thought of losing himself in an alcoholic stupor was appealing. Would the same staff be working there tonight? He decided it was worth the risk.

He pushed his way through the stoical smokers standing outside and entered the dimly lit bar, which had few customers, despite it being happy hour. Two trendy young men in business suits were sitting in a corner talking animatedly and drinking bottled beer, while an old man was studying the racing form up at the bar. A huge stuffed black bear oversaw proceedings from its position near the toilets. Joe got himself a pint and sat down at one of the small tables.

A middle-aged woman appeared through the front door in a cloud of sickly sweet perfume; she was wearing a very short dress under a posh-looking coat. Haughtily she cast her eyes around the bar as if searching for someone she knew, and with a swing of her hips, she made her way up to the bar. Joe felt embarrassed for the lady as she loudly ordered a Kick in the Balls cocktail. She turned round to survey the room again. Joe averted his eyes and tapped his wedding ring against his pint glass. Within seconds she downed the cocktail and, dabbing at her mouth with a tissue, she announced, 'Oh dear, I think I'm getting a bit drunk already.'

The old man at the bar glanced up briefly at her, then returned to his newspaper.

'I'd like another cocktail,' the woman said, looking around her. The barman rolled his eyes and he started putting the ingredients into the cocktail shaker. The woman, meanwhile, had fixed her gaze on the two young men in the corner.

The barman cleared his throat to get her attention as he set her fresh drink on the counter. The woman pulled out a wad of fifty pound notes.

'Oooops, sorry,' she said and giggled. 'I don't have anything smaller ... No, no wait. Here's a twenty.' She held it out between two fingers.

The barman took it without meeting her eyes, punched some buttons on the till and came back with her change. She took the tenner and dropped the remaining pound on the counter.

'Tip,' she said and smirked.

Shrugging, the barman dropped it in the Age Concern tin.

The young men in the corner were paying attention to the woman by this time. Joe could see them nudging each other and laughing, and he caught the word 'Milf' floating in the air. For a while, the woman stood at the bar drinking, switching to neat Scotch when she'd finished her cocktail and becoming noticeably unsteady on her feet. It was obvious that it was all a performance for the young fellas in the corner.

But they still didn't come over; they remained where they were, bawdily nudging each other and laughing. Joe cringed when he saw her trying to give them the kind of look that only teenagers gave each other across the school canteen table. When she got some change from her next drink she wandered over to the jukebox and selected a few tracks. She chose Rihanna's 'Umbrella', and had a little dance, drink in hand, while it played.

'Wheee!' she squealed as she gyrated in front of the jukebox. Everyone, even the old man, was looking at her now. She danced slowly towards the young men and set her drink down on their table.

'And what are you two conspiring about?' she asked in a low voice, trying to sound sexy.

'We were just admiring your dancing,' said one of the young men. He had dark blond hair, spiked stylishly on top, and a fashionable five o'clock shadow.

The woman squeezed herself into a seat between them. 'My name's Rebecca,' she said, holding out her hand first to the blond guy.

'Andy,' he said, shaking her hand. 'And this is Mark.' He nodded to his mate.

Mark, dark haired with a goatee beard, shook her hand. He caught Andy's eye and tried not to smile.

'Can I buy youse both a drink?' Rebecca asked.

Mark and Andy exchanged another glance. 'Yeah, sure. Why not, love,' said Mark. We're drinking Buds, thanks.'

Rebecca squeezed out past him and went up to the bar. She ordered a couple of bottles of Budweiser and another Kick in the Balls for herself.

Mark came up and joined her at the bar. 'Do you need a hand with those, love,' he said, sliding his arm around her waist. Joe saw him give her bum a quick squeeze, and as Rebecca turned round to face him he pulled her close and kissed her.

'Here love, my mate's after your pension!' called Andy from the corner and he broke into cackles of laughter. Even the barman tried to suppress a smile as he handed her back her change.

Rebecca prised herself away from Mark and blinked at him heavily. He started to laugh, then lifted the two bottles of beer and made his way back to the table. For a moment, Rebecca stood at the bar, swaying, cocktail in hand. Then she went over to the young men's table; they were deep in conversation and ignored her.

'C'mon, budge up,' she said chirpily.

They both looked up at her.

'Thanks for the beer, love, but don't you have people your own age to drink with?' said Mark.

'Aye, like that old boy up at the bar,' said Andy sniggering.

Rebecca's mouth fell open, and then closed again. She looked from Mark to Andy, took a huge gulp of her cocktail and stomped off to the ladies with the rest of it.

Joe was appalled. How could people be so cruel! He hoped the woman was all right. He had enough problems of his own without getting involved with strangers' problems though. He had come in to wet the baby's head – to celebrate the birth of his son – but somehow it didn't feel like something to celebrate. He'd gained a son but lost a wife.

'Bartender, I need a drink,' he shouted from his table.

'Of …?' asked the barman.

'Harp,' said Joe without giving it much thought. One drink was as good as another.

While the barman pulled his pint Joe remembered his father warning him never to be a 'lonely pint' – someone who sat drinking alone. He got up to pay the barman and sat down on a stool at the bar. The TV was on in the corner and Joe stayed there for the rest of the evening, knocking back pint after pint, numbing the pain in between each trip to the toilet. He became increasingly filled with self-loathing. 'Life is like this bar,' he declared to the barman while his seventh pint was being poured. 'It's somewhere you lose yourself, but it can never be your final destination.' People looked on, smiling. 'He's harmless,' someone said. Punters came and went, yet he remained.

A bell rang.

'Last orders, ladies and gentlemen,' called the barman.

Joe staggered out of the toilet and pushed his way through to the bar. Someone pushed him back; then a voice behind him threatened to give him a good kicking. Joe looked in his wallet: the last of his money was gone. It was a pity he wasn't as rich as that woman Rebecca who'd been flashing her cash earlier, he thought. He stuck his hand in the pocket of his jeans; he had enough loose change for a half pint and he shouted out his order.

'Half pints is for girls,' shouted a disembodied voice. Someone laughed.

Joe swayed forward and the half pint slipped from his hand and smashed on the floor. That seemed to cause even more laughter. The barman said something to the Italian waitress, who grabbed a mop and dustpan and came round to the front of the bar to clean up his mess.

Joe laid his hands flat on the bar and demanded another half.

'That'll be one eighty,' the barman said.

'But sure I dropped the last one. Are you not going to give me another?' Joe asked with a slow blink. 'I've no money left.'

'Yer getting no more!' the barman said, lifting the half and setting it back behind the counter. 'Go on – on yer bike. I think you've had enough for one night.'

'Ach well, you can't blame a man for trying,' Joe said and burped loudly. He slid down off his stool and, leaving his house keys lying in a puddle of spilt beer, he tried to focus on the front door. Like a pinball, he ricocheted off walls and people as he tried to get out. He'd started to hiccup and his legs felt as if they were going to give way under him.

'My wife had a baby today,' he told people as he passed them.

'Well done, mucker,' they said, slapping him on the back, propelling him towards the front door.

He felt invincible; he could do anything, go anywhere, fix anything. He'd find another job! No bother! He tried to snap his fingers. Joe fell out of the bar and staggered off in the general direction of home

* * *

It was beautiful outside. The city streets were carpeted with snow, much of it fresh and unblemished, and strangely, it didn't feel cold. Joe had one thought – to get some cash. He reached an ATM but his hands were shaking. Was it cold? An elderly man with a dog stopped in front of him. Joe was sure he'd seen the man somewhere before.

'Here, could you get some money out of the machine for me?' He shoved his bank card into the man's hand. 'My pin number is zero-zero-four-eight.'

The old man frowned and shook his head. His dog sniffed Joe's leg.

'Please,' said Joe, 'I need to get a taxi back to the hospital. My wife had a baby today – a baby boy.' Joe couldn't help grinning from ear to ear.

'Congratulations, sir,' said the old man. 'But you really shouldn't go handing out your card and pin number to strangers! … And do you think it's a good idea to go to the hospital in your state?'

Joe knelt down and stroked the wee dog, giving him his best smile. The dog wagged his tail. 'Aye, maybe you're right about that,' he said. 'I just wanted to wet the baby's head. I think I might have overdone it a bit.' He grinned up at the old man.

'Sir, I'll get you a taxi,' the old man said and he waved his stick at one that was passing by.

It slowed down and pulled over, but just as Joe lunged for the door handle the taxi suddenly drove off, leaving him scrabbling on the pavement. 'Ignorant … galoot,' he yelled from the gutter. The dog licked his face.

'Where do you live? Maybe I can help you get home. I'm Walter from Helen's café, by the way. I've seen you in there several times.'

Joe stood up and squinted at Walter. Yes, that's where he knew him from! Walter and the interesting lady. He mumbled his address, and repeated it as if he was afraid he'd forget. Walter waved down another taxi and spoke to the driver.

'Well, if you know him and are sure,' the driver said through the open window.

The back door of the car opened and Joe found himself in the warm, plush interior of a Mercedes. Joe gave him his address.

'Do you have money?' the driver
asked. Joe told him his date of birth.

'Do. You. Have. Money?' the driver repeated.

'I'll pay,' Walter said, handing him a twenty pound note. 'Will that cover it?'

'Aye, that'll do it all right … Dear, oh dear,' said the driver looking in his rear-view mirror. 'Listen mate, if you feel sick wind down the bloomin' window!'

They drove off, the lurching bumpy car ride doing nothing for Joe's head or stomach. When they arrived at Joe's house, he practically fell out the back door of the car.

'Sorry, I can't give you any change out of money the old man gave me,' the driver said, not even bothering to pretend he'd looked. He rolled his eyes at Joe, leaned back to close the door and drove off, leaving Joe swaying outside his own gate.

He trudged through the snow to his front door and, hanging on to the brass letter box, looked for his keys. Where were his keys? He followed his own footsteps back down the driveway. Maybe they'd dropped out of his pocket. He hoped they hadn't fallen out in the taxi. When he didn't find them he decided that, since it was such a nice night, he'd sleep out. He slumped down in the porch, his head dropping to his chest.

He was awoken by a jingling noise. For a moment he wondered if it was Santa Claus. Then he smiled to himself. His keys were unlocking the door without him doing anything! God was on his side! He looked up and saw a young skinny girl, somehow familiar, unlocking his front door.

* * *

Wiara had seen his keys lying on the bar counter and had picked up enough information from his rambling conversation to know where he lived. She had brought them to him but hadn't been expecting to find him in this state. Not to worry, as the Irish said – she knew what to do. Straining, she hauled him into the house, and once she'd got him settled on a sofa, she flicked on the gas heating; it rumbled like an angry God.

She may have been a slim girl but she was strong. As a child, she had helped her father build their new home, hauling slabs of bricks, lifting and carrying – doing whatever was needed. It had been hard – not just hard work, but hard because she never had much time for her friends who wanted to party all the time. Still, now it meant she was able to save this man, heavy with unconsciousness.

She would stay and look after him. She knew his wife was in hospital and he was all alone. She lifted a rug and, whirling it in the air, watched it balloon and fall over him. Then she tucked him in, cocooning him on the settee like a newborn. The man instantly began to snore.

Wiara inspected what she immediately decided was her new home. She had travelled far enough to find it.

* * *

The heaviness of a blanket fell over his shoulders. He could feel the heat. He dreamt that he was surrounded by fire, his clothes burning off and leaving him naked in front of his mates. The flames got closer and there seemed to be no escape. Then a young girl swaddled him in a blanket to protect him from the inferno and led him from the building.

* * *

Slowly, Joe awakened. Light was sneaking into the room around the closed curtains and he could hear the musical sound of children's laughter outside. Feck! Late for work for the first time in his life! Joe swore as he tried to get up. He only got as far as sitting upright. The first thing he saw was the waitress from the bar – what was her name? She was surveying him from a chair at the end of the sofa.

He struggled to remember what had happened. Why was she there? Was he still in the bar? He glanced about him – familiar blue striped wallpaper, Diane's sparkling crystal collection in a cabinet. He was in his own living room. He pulled the rug tightly around him, as if it would protect him from himself, and stared at the girl. She had an unusual heart-shaped face, accentuated by her short haircut, and her eyes gleamed.

He poked her with his finger to see if she was real. 'Jesus, sweet Jesus,' he said when she flinched. He checked under the blanket to see if he still had his trousers on. He'd never blacked-out before. What was he doing with a child who couldn't be more than – what, seventeen?

The girl smiled. 'I'm not that easy!' she said.

Joe blushed, much to her amusement. 'You're the waitress from the bar!' he said. 'What are you doing here?'

'You left your keys there, so I came to find you,' she explained, her English heavily accented. 'Good thing, too. You'd fallen asleep outside. It was very cold.'

'Thank you … I'm sorry, I can't remember your name.'

The girl grinned, revealing slightly crooked white teeth. 'Wiara. It means "faith".'

'It doesn't sound Italian.'

'It's not. I'm Polish … but I can speak Italian. People are more likely to hire an Italian than a Pole.'

Joe recalled Kilwinner's words in the bar that night. 'I'm Joe,' he said. 'Joe Lonely.'

'Hello, Joe Lonely,' she said and proffered her hand as if she were transacting a business deal. She held his gaze. 'The priest says that we're all unique and everyone has a role to play. Maybe I played mine last night. You think, Mr Lonely?'

Joe blushed again and wondered at it. He hadn't blushed for years!

Chapter 25

Thursday 10th November
They needed the hospital bed, so Diane and baby Tom were packed up and sent home. The baby was safely strapped into the back of the car with Diane beside him. She just sat there, solemnly holding a white plastic bag with 'HOSPITAL' written on it and looking out the window at the passing houses and cars.

'There's someone staying with us – a friend,' Joe said. He pumped his horn at a car that darted out in front of him and immediately glanced backwards to ensure it hadn't disturbed the baby. Tom was happily gurgling and kicking his feet in the air; Diane kept her head turned away, devoid of any emotion, never mind concern for her child. This was not the woman Joe knew and loved.

'Her name's Wiara. It means "faith" in Polish,' Joe explained. 'She's only seventeen and works in a local pub.'

In his rear-view mirror, Joe saw Diane turn to look at him, frown, then go back to staring out the window again.

'We're going to be okay,' he assured her. 'We'll get through this in one piece. We will.'

When they arrived at the house, Joe carried Tom to the front door, but before he had the chance to put his key in the lock the door opened and Wiara appeared, all smiles and greetings. Her eyes went straight to the carry cot and in that instant, Joe could see she had fallen in love with the child. That's how Helen should be, Joe couldn't help thinking. Wiara took the child from him and carried him into the warmth of the living room.

Diane was still sitting in the back of the car, a blank expression on her face. Joe ran back to help her out, opening an umbrella as he went. The rain was coming down in sheets and the wind caught the underside of the umbrella, blowing it inside out. Diane didn't seem to care as her hair got soaked and clung to her face like rat's tails.

Zombie-like, she made her way towards the house and showed no signs of recognition when she stepped inside. Their home had once been her palace; now, she might as well still be in the hospital for all the interest she showed. Wiara pecked Diane on the cheek by way of a greeting, but Diane's eyes remained dull and blank.

Joe closed the door behind them, carrying the rest of their bags into the hallway. Without a word, Diane went upstairs and Joe found her later, fully clothed, lying on the bed in the darkness. She didn't acknowledge his presence. He lay beside her and held her hand.

'It'll be okay,' he said softly. 'Everything will be okay.'

* * *

Joe opened the front door, its hinges squealing like Tom's cries.

'Father Michael is away. I fill,' the priest said in a Polish accent.

Joe ushered him into the house. Wiara smiled at the priest as she bottle-fed Tom, pacing up and down the living room. Joe and the priest went upstairs to Diane's bedroom.

A short time later the red-faced priest reappeared. 'I think I do no good. I'll pray for her. The baby. I'll pray for you.'

Later, the doorbell rang. Joe answered it.

'I'm the locum,' said a young man. 'I'm here to see someone called Diane.' After a short while, he left too. 'I think your wife needs psychiatric help. I've seen this kind of thing before. Here's a prescription for antidepressants, though I doubt they'll help. I'll put her down as an emergency.'

The next day, there was a loud rap on the letterbox. Joe opened the front door.

After a quick examination the Community Psychiatric Nurse said, 'I'll put her onto a waiting list.'

'But she's an emergency case,' said Joe.

'It might seem like an emergency to *you*, but it's not to her,' the nurse said.

Later that day, a counsellor showed up. 'She needs to want to change. Get her to make the appointment herself next time,' he said.

'Don't worry – I'll help,' said Wiara.

Tom began to cry.

Joe closed the door.

* * *

Wiara, dressed demurely in faded blue denim jeans and a crisp white shirt, carried the child into Joe and Diane's room and settled him in his cot. She was such a blessing. She had arrived at just the right time in their lives. Clucking and cooing, she tended to the child and tucked him in for his nap, then took Diane's half-eaten lunch away.

Joe was sitting in the chair beside the cot looking at his wife. Despite her depressed and unwashed state, he loved her more than ever. He knew that soon she would see Tom as a gift, not a burden, but he wished it would happen quickly. The counsellor had insisted that Diane be put under no stress, but he really wanted his wife back.

'What are you staring at?' Diane asked from the bed. 'You're probably thinking of ways to get rid of me.' Her words hung in the room. Then she went on, unable to keep the sarcasm out of her voice: 'You probably want to find yourself someone else … Oh yeah, you already have.'

Joe placed a comforting hand on her shoulder. 'No. You're my girl. There's no one else for me.'

'You hate me.'

He lay down beside her. 'I don't! I love you!'

She pushed him away with surprising strength. 'I don't believe you.'

Joe sat up on the edge of the bed, his back to Diane so she couldn't see his face. 'I need to tell you something,' he said quietly.

'See! I knew it. She can have you, for all I care – and the baby too.'

He shook his head. 'I've lost my job,' he said.

Silence sliced between them again.

167

'When did this happen?' Diane eventually asked, not a shred of sympathy in her voice.

'The day Tom was
born.' 'You never said.'

'You'd other things to worry about.'

'So what are we going to do?'

'Well, I'll sign on … and I'll go down to the Job Centre and see what they have going.'

'The national begging bowl!' she said with disgust.

'I've paid my taxes and I'm entitled,' Joe said, feeling more exhausted than after any day's work. 'I'm no scrounger.'

'And how can we afford Wiara?'

Joe hung his head. 'She's helping. She's happy to, if we give her a roof over her head.'

'She's replacing me,' said Diane matter-of-factly and turned away from Joe to face the wall.

Joe closed the door quietly behind him when he left the room.

Chapter 26

The Jobs and Benefits Office looked like a bunker with its grey concrete walls and flat, windowless facade. Mothers stood around outside smoking, their pale youngsters in push chairs sucking on sugar, hardened looks already forming on their chubby faces.

Joe went in past the bouncer on the door and cast about for where to go. He couldn't help noticing the state of disrepair and decay. The walls needed replastered and a good lick of fresh paint. The only splash of colour was the 'Jobs and Benefits' sign itself.

He entered the Job Zone – how trendy, he thought – in which disparate people milled around computers, or sat in long rows of chairs. The last time he had been in a place like this there were little typed cards on the wall. One minute you were sixteen and the next you were fifty. Places like this measured the passage of time in a way that was hard to stomach. There had been few enough opportunities for apprentices when he was sixteen; what would it be like for him now!

He asked for directions to sign on and soon found himself in a large grey room that hadn't been decorated since the 1970s, all brown, cream and orange with tatty filthy chairs, stretching the length of the room and bolted to the floor. Opposite the rows of chairs were rows of booths, each with its own queue, like rat's tails wriggling across the floor.

'Why didn't you come in earlier,' a disembodied voice demanded of a woman in the queue closest to Joe.

The woman, who looked like she was in her 30s and had piercings in every visible part of her body, folded her arms across her chest. 'Sinuses!' she stated and snorted to emphasise her point.

Joe suddenly felt like having a shower, a very hot one that would cleanse him of this place. He'd do anything rather than have to show up here again. Then he heard a familiar voice call his name.

'Lonely Joe! That's a fine mane of black hair you've got!'

Joe lifted his head to look at a balding man sitting behind the desk of the grey booth at which he was queuing. He'd no idea who he was!

'Surely I haven't changed that much?!' the man asked, raising his eyebrows. 'Though right enough, we haven't seen each other in thirty years.'

'Dennis Breach!' Joe blurted out. An image of a plump teenager came to mind.

'Aye, that's me. Working in the dole office for my sins. As I recall, you couldn't wait to get out of school, get yourself a trade. You're probably making more money in a week than I do in a month!'

Joe sat down in front of him, feeling like a pupil in the headmaster's office – ashamed and guilty, even though he'd done nothing wrong.

'Anyway, what're doing here?' Dennis asked. 'Probably looking for more contractor work.'

Joe crumpled up his application to sign on and dropped his head. Then he remembered Diane and Tom. There was no place for pride. He flattened out the form and slid it under the Perspex screen towards his former classmate.

Dennis reddened when he saw it. 'Oh, right! Listen, I'm off for my tea break. It was good to see you again.' He smiled awkwardly, then signalled to a colleague and left.

A man who replaced him smelled of big macs and was so large he made the chair he was sitting on look as if it was no bigger than a pinhead. He took Joe's form and started laboriously keying the information into the computer in front of him, checking the details with Joe as he went. His fat fingers kept making mistakes and he had to retype almost everything at least once.

'Now you know, don't you, that you won't get any money for twenty-six weeks,' the big man said when he got to the end. 'New rules.'

'What?!' Joe shouted, astonished. 'But I've paid taxes since I was sixteen. I've never even had a day off sick.'

'The rules are that if you resign or are terminated …'

'Fired, you mean?'

'Yes … then you're not entitled to anything for twenty-six weeks. Anything else?' The man splayed his flabby fingers on the desk to signal the end of the meeting.

Joe wanted to yell, 'What the hell am I supposed to do? I have a wife, a new baby and a mortgage in negative equity.' But what was the point. He'd never felt so demoralised in his life. Losing his job was bad enough, but to discover he was a failure at getting state benefits was too much. For the first time in his life, he realised how fragile life was; no one was more than a millimetre away from financial ruin.

As he drove away from the dole office, he worked it out in his head. Twenty-six weeks was about six and a half months. He reckoned they had enough money left for the basics for one month. What the hell would they do after that? He'd have to find a new job – any job. He understood now how tempting it would be to turn to crime. He thought about Tom and imagined the baby staring at him hungrily, his little arms outstretched. He felt very tired, very tired indeed.

Chapter 27

Soon the rejections were rolling in.

We're looking for someone a bit different.

We're looking for someone a bit younger.

We'll let you know.

Most applicants are school leavers.

Your application was unsuccessful.

It's a buyers' market. What with the recession …

We only take the best.

Do you have experience in anything other than construction?

At one agency they didn't bother to tone down their giggles as they marked the test that Joe had taken. He knew why. 'Dumbo 2011,' someone whispered behind the screen. Joe swallowed. I've a new born baby, he thought.

Thank you for your time. We'll let you know.

He suddenly felt ancient at the age of fifty. Was he going to have to beg?

When you're responsible for other people it makes you do things you never thought you would.

* * *

Joe parked his car in his usual spot. He ached for the routine and order of his former life. He missed it badly. He checked his watch, got out of the car and returned to the building site.

Billy was climbing down the scaffolding outside one of the houses. He yelled something to one of the other men, and then laughed at the reply. It had been a long time since Joe had laughed.

Kilwinner's office on the corner of the site was one of those grey prefab boxes which he'd kitted out with good heating and comfortable chairs. Joe half hoped no one would be there today, but he could hear the din of voices coming from within. He knocked and moments later, the Governor opened the door.

'What the hell do you want?' he asked Joe gruffly.

'I need to speak to the boss.' Joe said, glancing past him and seeing Kilwinner sitting with his feet up on his desk and a few pin-ups of Page Three girls on the walls.

'You talk to *me*,' the Governor said, drawing himself up to his full height.

'I need my job back.'

A big grin split the Governor's face. 'Here, boss! Have you heard this,' he said over his shoulder into the office. 'It's Lonely Joe wanting his job back!'

Kilwinner mumbled something that Joe couldn't make out. Then the Governor turned back to him. 'Wait here,' he said and slammed the door closed.

Joe stood outside and waited. Minutes turned into half an hour. Occasionally, one of the men on site looked over and pointed, calling out to another colleague, 'Look who it is!'

A further twenty-five minutes went by. Joe was foundered; he was walking around stomping his feet to try to stay warm. Suddenly the office door swung open.

'Get in here,' the Governor ordered.

Joe stepped into what seemed like a sauna and felt the panic rise when the door was shut, muffling the sounds of the building site. Kilwinner was leaning back in his chair, feet on his desk, hands behind his head, glaring at Joe.

'I'm kinda busy at the moment, Lonely.' He swept his hand in the air above the papers that were lying on his desk. 'So hurry up and get on with it. What do you want?'

'I'd like to come back to work.'

The phone rang. 'I need to take this. Wait outside,' Kilwinner said, snapping his fingers and picking up phone.

Joe stumbled back out into the cold air again. More of his former workmates had gathered near the hut and were nudging each other and smiling. One man with whom he'd previously had an altercation took off his hat and walked past him laughing.

Joe focused his thoughts on his son's smile and waited … and waited. Another half hour went by. It was starting to get dark. Just as the men were knocking off for the day, Kilwinner emerged. He'd timed it perfectly. The men gathered round for the performance.

'So you want your job back!' Kilwinner said, playing to the crowd. 'You're an arrogant bastard, Lonely – no respect for your betters. But if you apologise I might consider it.'

'I'm a good worker,' was all Joe could say, unable to keep the desperation out of his voice.

Kilwinner narrowed his eyes at him. 'See! You can't even take a simple instruction. There's only one boss and that's Kilwinner.' He pointed at his own chest. 'I need an apology … and if you ask me nicely for your job back – say "please" and everything – you might see that my heart isn't the swinging brick people think it is.'

Joe hesitated. He'd been trying to fix Tom's face in his mind's eye, but it was immediately replaced by an image of him beating Kilwinner with a sledgehammer. Taken aback by the violence of his thoughts, Joe turned to leave.

'Shove it,' he said. 'I'd rather clean toilets!'

'Get out of here before I set the Governor on you, Lonely,' Kilwinner hollered, 'AND DON'T COME BACK.'

Joe got back into his car and rested his forehead on the steering wheel for a few minutes. What was he going to do?

Suddenly, someone opened the back door of his car and got in.

'Twenty-nine Westbroke Close, please. Bloody hell, it's freezing out there!' the man said, rubbing his hand together.

Joe stared at him in his rear-view mirror. He'd never seen him before in his life!

'Sorry mate, are you booked?' the man asked.

Joe turned round and gave him a puzzled look. 'I was just heading home,' he said.

The man grappled with the door handle. 'Jesus, sorry mate. I thought you were a taxi.' He fell out of the car and walked off into the night.

Joe sat and thought about it for a minute. It wasn't a bad idea – better than nothing. He might as well earn a few quid from the car, the only real asset he had. He envied taxi drivers: they'd no prick of a boss, no one to fire them. Taxi drivers had status; his parents had regarded them as professional as a doctor or dentist. God, he wished he had his parents to talk to now.

* * *

Wiara's beautiful eyes shone brightly while she fed Tom. When he'd finished his bottle, she burped him and began to sing. Her voice worked like magic on the baby, his eyes closing and his breathing slowing down as he drifted off into a contented sleep. She took him upstairs to his cot. She was going to be a stunner in a few years time and would make a wonderful mother, Joe thought when she returned to the kitchen to put his dinner in the microwave. Wiara had brought happiness and turmoil to his life in equal measure. Joe didn't know his wife anymore; he didn't know what he'd do without Wiara.

In the morning his whole body ached. Sleeping on the sofa wasn't doing much for his back. He switched on the TV and listened to the news about thousands of unemployed and how the government was going to crack down on cheaters and idlers. He went into the kitchen to get a cup of tea and slumped down in a chair, his head in his hands. He couldn't get a job, his wife hated him, he had a child he couldn't support and a young girl who was staying with them out of pity. He had come to dread the arrival of the postman each day: there seemed to be nothing but rejection letters and bills. And there was nothing but rejection from his wife; she'd stopped eating, a protest against … against what, he wasn't quite sure.

Just then, he heard gentle music coming from the living room. Like a man possessed he drifted in its direction. When he went into the room, the beautiful sad music enveloped him and swirled around in his head. He felt a gentle hand touch his shoulder and, closing his eyes, he imagined that Diane had returned to her old self. He found himself embracing her and they began to dance.

'The music is magical,' Joe whispered in her ear.

'We play this song when we need to remember what we have to be thankful for,' she said, holding Joe close. 'Although much of life may have passed, much of great value remains.'

'I know, I still have so much – a beautiful wife and child, and we've a roof over our heads … But I'm old and useless now. I can't support what little I have left.'

The melancholy song finished and Joe opened his eyes. He was holding Wiara in his arms, not Diane, and he recoiled.

'Why do you push me away?' Wiara asked, her beautiful eyes bright with a fire that he had once seen in Diane's.

'I've things to do,' Joe said, embarrassed and he rushed to get out of the room.

Just then, Tom wailed; Wiara went tend to him.

* * *

Diane had heard the music and lay in bed listening to it. The little witch Wiara was casting some kind of spell over her husband and she was powerless to stop her. She pulled the thick quilt up over her head. Sleep was the only respite she got.

Then the imposter child started to cry.

Chapter 28

The café doorbell tinkled as Joe stomped in, kicking the snow off his boots on the doorstep. Helen looked exasperated. She was probably wondering why he was spending so much time in her café. He felt like shouting at her, 'I want to work, but no one will employ a fifty-year-old builder with no references.'

He sat at his usual table by the door and began reading his newspaper. Walter glanced at Joe and nodded. Why's he nodding at me, Joe wondered. Then the taxi incident came flooding back. Helen came over immediately, holding her ordering pad and took his order for an Ulster fry. But she continued to hover around his table. Joe wondered what she wanted.

'One fried egg?' she asked him eventually while watching the old couple closely.

'No, two,' he replied, becoming as interested in Walter and Margaret's conversation as she was.

'No sausages?'

'Two sausages,' Joe said quickly, tapping his hard hat that sat on the table.

With that, Helen wandered over to Walter and Margaret's table and collected their dishes. The old couple stopped talking and Joe went back to his reading.

'Don't you two duckies look nice together?' he heard Helen say to them.

Joe wished he could cut two eye-holes in his paper. For some reason he was interested in this old couple and the story that was playing out in front of him. It felt significant, like he was in the theatre and he might learn something from them. Or maybe he was grasping at straws, trying to find meaning where there was none.

'Could we have ...' Walter began.

'… two more cups of Auntie Helen's special brew?' Helen laughed. 'That'll soon knock the cold outta the pair of ya.'

'We're too old to have aunties,' said Margaret.

Joe heard a jingling noise and, peeping round the corner of his newspaper, he saw the old man's dog by the door having a good shake. It reminded Joe of a childhood pet.

'You're never too old to have aunties. The tea's on me,' Helen said.

Joe let his paper slip so he had a better view round the café. What was Helen playing at, he wondered.

Margaret and Walter looked at each other and smiled. The dog lay down at their feet, his nose between his paws. A few moments later, Helen returned with their teas, hovering nearby after she'd set them down on the table.

Helen is more nosy than Diane, Joe thought. He wished she'd give them a break – some privacy. In any case, he wanted his fry!

'Well … just shout if you need anything,' Helen said, eventually going back behind her counter.

Joe watched Margaret give Walter a photograph. It seemed to have two people in it. 'He'd never liked the word "husband",' Margaret said.

Walter examined the picture but said nothing.

'Now I think I know why,' Margaret went on. 'It probably pricked his conscience. What a hypocrite. I remember him going to Bible study. And I remember the contempt he treated me with.'

'You use the word "remember" a lot,' Walter said. 'I know memories are sometimes all people of our age have, but it need not always be the case. We can make new memories of our own.'

Joe wanted to tell them about his memories and how he longed to make good ones for his son.

'Yes, you're right, Walter,' Margaret said, 'and I'm feeling better on the outside. Really. But I need to know who she was and if they had children.'

Walter frowned. 'Margaret, might I suggest that that might not be very helpful? It's not what has happened in the past that's important now, it's what can happen in the future. It's the future that's important … There I've said it.'

Joe silently put down his cup and closed his eyes.

'The future?' asked Margaret.

They were old, with nothing to look forward to, yet here they were talking about the future. Joe felt momentarily ashamed for feeling so sorry for himself. He had everything ahead of him.

'While I prayed in the hospital church I came to realise just what was most important,' Walter said.

Margaret rubbed an ear and frowned, as if finding it difficult to understand what he was saying. Then she said, 'I need to lay a ghost to rest before I go thinking about the future.'

'I've had my share of … ghosts,' Walter said. 'I heard a song on the radio not long ago. I think I was here at the time. It went something like 'You've got stuck in a moment and you can't get out of it', and I knew that was me. Before I met you, I thought being alive meant just breathing. But being alive is so much more than that.'

Joe was dying to interrupt them. He wanted to tell them that he thought they were two of the loveliest people he'd ever met. He imagined that if his own parents were still alive, they'd be like Walter and Margaret.

Margaret rubbed her hands, clearing perplexed by Walter's words. 'But I need to know the truth,' she said. 'I deserve to know the truth about my past.'

Yes she did, thought Joe. My wife needs to know the truth too. She needs to know that I love her and that she is needed.

'I'm worried that that might not be the best course of action. But it goes without saying that I'll support you, whatever you do.'

Joe watched Walter rub his arm as he said this. There was something about the way he did it. Something wasn't right.

Margaret nodded and smiled. 'Thank you. That means a great deal. You're so unlike anybody I've ever met.'

Just then, the dog whined a little and stood up. He stretched out his front paws, his bottom in the air, and yelped. Joe frowned.

Even the poor dog was old. Yet even the dog had an air of dignity about him.

'It's time to go and find out the truth,' Margaret said.

As they rose from their table, Joe quickly hid behind his newspaper. He wondered when they'd be back again. He wanted to know what happened next.

Chapter 29

Over the Christmas holidays Joe had thought a lot about Walter, Margaret and their little dog. He'd wondered how they were, and if Margaret had found out the truth and laid some ghosts to rest.

He'd come to the café today just to get out of the house. But he also hoped he'd see Margaret and Walter and be able to catch up with their story. It seemed he'd picked a good day to come.

The old couple were sitting at their usual table holding hands. Clearly they'd become closer over the holidays. But the air was tense. The dog was hiding under their table; even Helen was keeping her distance behind the counter. Margaret was looking well though. She'd had her hair done and she seemed to be wearing new clothes.

As usual, Joe was listening from behind his newspaper. Idly he wondered how hard it would be to get work as a spy, or a private detective.

'I hate when things are so ... so ... up in the air,' Margaret said. 'I do too,' said Walter. 'I do too. But even oldies like us can adjust.'

'You cheer me up, even ... even when I'm probably going to lose everything.' There was a pause. 'Am I wrong to hope this will turn out okay?' Margaret asked.

Joe wondered what they had planned. It sounded like they were waiting for something – or someone.

'I wonder how my battle will go?'

'I'll look out for you, Margaret. If they want to hurt you they'll have to get through Ted and me first. That's right, isn't it Ted?'

Why would anyone want to hurt Margaret, Joe wondered. He'd look out for her too, if he was given half a chance.

'You two dearies want me to clear your cups away?' Helen asked from behind the counter. 'And maybe Ted would like a sausage.'

Joe heard the dog chomping happily on his sausage while the old couple argued fondly over who would pay.

'That part of your life is over,' he heard Walter reassure Margaret. 'Those people who've made your life such a misery until now don't matter, and Ted and I will be with you to help you sort them out, once and for all.'

Joe took a sip of his tea and turned the page of his newspaper. He wasn't reading a word of it; what was happening in the café was much more interesting.

'But I'm afraid it's all going to go wrong … between us, I mean,' Margaret said. 'I couldn't go back to that – to having nothing. If I hadn't met you I would just have existed – but I don't think that would be good enough now. Breathing isn't living.'

'It wouldn't be good enough for me either anymore. You're … beautiful. Have I told you that lately?'

'Who looks at old women?'

'Old men.'

'You should have gone to Specsavers!'

Joe couldn't stop himself from laughing and turned it into a cough, spluttering tea all over the table. Helen came over with his fry and set it down on the table. But just then, he sensed the atmosphere change and seconds later the bell on the door of the café jingled.

In came … the drunk woman from the bar? Joe blinked and tried to remember it. Yes, it had been the night his son was born. Rebecca, that was her name. She'd been flinging her money around, drinking cocktails and making a fool of herself. So this was Margaret's Rebecca! He suddenly realised he'd been staring and that he'd put far too much ketchup on his chips. But no one seemed to notice, so he gave up the pretence of minding his own business.

Helen stood behind the counter, her arms folded, almost daring Rebecca to say something nasty. Rebecca made her way over to

Walter and Margaret's table and stood staring at them for a while. Walter wearily held her gaze. Margaret shrunk into herself.

Rebecca pointed at Walter. 'What has this to do with your fancy man?' she asked Margaret.

Joe would love to be regarded as a fancy man at Walter's age, he thought.

Walter tipped his cap and stood up. 'Won't you join me and my wife-to-be?'

Joe almost choked. So, the old couple were going to get married!

Without losing her composure, Rebecca set a document down on the table in front of Margaret. 'Let's keep this brief and painless,' she said. 'Just sign here' – she pointed – 'and then I can get on with my life.'

So that was Rebecca's game!

Walter said, 'I don't...'

'... I don't have my reading glasses with me,' Margaret interrupted. 'I suppose this is the deed you wanted me to sign earlier?'

'Sign!' Rebecca ordered.

'I don't have a pen,' said Margaret.

Rebecca rummaged around in her bag and produced a fancy gold pen.

Joe took a deep breath and held it. What would Margaret do?

'Ma'am, my solicitor will look this over and get back to you,' Walter said, putting himself between Margaret and Rebecca.

Good on you Walter, thought Joe. He knew that if he was needed he'd step in to help too.

Rebecca narrowed her eyes and became very flushed. She scowled at Walter and brought her face up close to his. Walter looked rather alarmed at such confrontational behaviour from a woman. Even the dog sensed it and began to growl under the table.

'I'll have that bloody dog put down,' snarled Rebecca. 'This is none of your business. This is family business – and the family is all here.'

'Margaret and I are getting married,' Walter announced. 'Ted and me' – he gestured towards the dog – '*we're* Margaret's family.'

Joe cheered inside his head. You tell her, Walter.

Rebecca hesitated momentarily. 'Do you think men really like you, you worthless old cow?' she said to Margaret. 'This crafty old bugger's only after the house.'

Joe gasped at the ferocity and bitterness of her words. He was having to work hard to keep his temper in check. He didn't want what had happened with his old boss to happen again here. He didn't want to be barred from Helen's café.

'I assure you, men most certainly do like your mother,' Walter said, stepping between the two women again. 'In fact, this man loves your mother. I'm deeply honoured that she has accepted my proposal of marriage. I would've preferred us all to be friends, but I will not tolerate you insulting her. You must apologise immediately.'

Rebecca stamped her foot. Joe could feel the anger rising in him. He was more outraged by Rebecca's behaviour than he'd ever been by Kilwinner's.

'You're forcing me to do this,' Rebecca shouted. 'Forcing me. I'm only being cruel to be kind.'

'Where are the twins?' Margaret asked.

There was a resounding silence. Joe had stopped eating or pretending to read his newspaper. He was sitting on the edge of his seat, ready to pitch in if necessary.

'Not far away,' Rebecca said. 'Everybody is here.' She waved her hand at the window.

Seconds later, the bell of the café door jangled again. In came a tall, well-built man wearing an expensive suit, sparkling cuff links and well-polished shoes. He was accompanied by a neat, prim woman with two children – twins, Joe thought.

'Walter, let me introduce you,' Margaret said. 'This is Rebecca's husband Blake, my two grandchildren Michael and Martin – and you've already encountered my husband's other wife Grainne.' She paused and then said more loudly, 'This is Walter, my husband-to-be.'

Blake thrust out his hand towards Walter. At least he has some manners, thought Joe.

But Walter wasn't having any of it. 'You won't mind if I don't shake your hand, sir,' he said and put his hands in his coat pockets.

Joe cheered inside his head again.

Blake didn't look put out in the slightest. Instead, he pointed at the table. 'Tea anyone,' he asked, looking round at them all.

Joe kept his head down; this guy was like Kilwinner and the Governor rolled into one.

'We're all out of tea,' Helen retorted from behind the counter.

'Coffee then.' Blake snapped his fingers.

'We're all out of coffee too.'

'Damn right,' Joe mumbled and set his cutlery down with a rattle. It took all his willpower to stay in his seat. Men like Blake really got up his nose. Who did he think he was, coming in here and throwing his weight around.

Walter went over and stood beside Margaret. 'We'll take our leave, Margaret,' he said, helping her to her feet.

Once Margaret was standing up, she turned to Rebecca and said, 'Why?'

'You're asking why I hate you? You're like an old woman in the market who sells fish. I was laughed at when I was a child. I didn't know how to do anything properly.' Joe could hardly believe the venom that was coming from Rebecca's mouth. 'And that whole make do and mend thing! Bloody hell!' Rebecca went on. 'Why should I have to struggle? I want the best for myself and my children. I want a nice house, nice clothes, nice friends. You never gave me any of that.'

'Watch your language! Any more of that and I'll have to ask you to leave. You're disturbing the customers,' Helen said, looking at Joe.

Joe nodded, grateful to Helen for stepping in. He wasn't sure how much longer he could keep quiet.

'I'm tired of waiting, Becky,' Blake said gruffly. 'Just hurry up and get the old cow to sign.'

'Of course she'll sign, Blake. Just hold on,' Rebecca said before going over to Margaret and handing her the pen. 'Sign,' she ordered.

'This is intolerable. Be off with the lot of you,' Walter said. The dog growled under the table.

Blake glared at Walter. 'You'd want to control that animal. I'll have it put down. It's frightening the children.'

'You're doing that all by yourself, sir!' Walter said, waving his walking stick in the air.

'You old ...' Blake snarled. 'I hope I haven't come all this way to be disappointed, Becky ... GET HER TO SIGN THE DAMN PAPER!' Then he pushed Walter, who lost his balance and fell back onto a chair.

'Walter! Are you okay?' Margaret gasped.

Ted came out from under the table, snapping at Blake. The twins started to cry. Rebecca was shoving the pen in Margaret's face and screaming at her to sign.

'I'll protect you Margaret!' Walter wheezed, waving his stick in the air.

Suddenly Joe banged his fist on his table. 'They'll be no more of this!'

Everyone fell silent.

'This café is closed!' said Helen, coming out from behind the counter.

Blake fumbled for the door handle as Joe strode towards him.

'It's okay, I'm going ... I'm going,' Blake said, waving his hands in front of him. 'I might have known you'd get it wrong, Becky!' he called over his shoulder as he wrenched the door of the café open. 'I don't want to hear from you or have anything to do with those little brats again!'

'Wait, darling,' Rebecca shouted. 'Please don't go. I'll get her to sign ... Blake?'

For the first time, Joe felt sorry for Rebecca. He went back to his seat but he'd completely lost his appetite.

'Wait,' Margaret said to Rebecca. 'You forgot this.' She signed the document and handed it back to Rebecca. 'You can keep the house and every stick of furniture in it, especially that stupid desk,' Margaret went on. 'That house was a prison to me and I don't want to be reminded of how I wasted my years. You can have everything. I don't care. I'll be living with Walter from now on.'

Walter smiled.

'Thank you,' Rebecca said, checking the signature. Then she left.

* * *

Five minutes later, Joe left the café to go home. He heard angry shouting coming from some waste groundnearby. He went to see what was going on.

There stood Rebecca and Blake yelling at each other.

'Quit your slabbering!' Blake shouted at her.

'You're nothing but a worthless piece of shit,' she hissed into his face.

These two were once married to each other! Joe was incredulous. He suddenly realised things at home weren't so bad after all.

Then Blake grabbed Rebecca by the throat and squeezed. Joe didn't much like Rebecca but he couldn't stand by and watch her be killed by this bully. So he ran at Blake with his hard hat, clocking the man across the face with it several times until Blake collapsed to the ground. For a moment, no one moved. Then Rebecca got stuck into Blake, kicking him for all she was worth, and laughing while she did it.

Joe phoned for an ambulance and the police. He'd never seen anything so vicious.

Rebecca took off her wedding ring and flung it into the bushes at the back.

Chapter 30

Joe sat at his wife's bedside; his son lay in the cot next to him. He loved them both so much. Diane had her back to him.

Joe began talking, telling her about everything that had been going on the past couple of months since their son was born. He told her about Margaret and Walter and their dog, the troubles they had and how they weren't giving up, even though they were in their seventies. They didn't have money or a perfect life; they had nothing except each other and that was enough. He told her about his own troubles – about not being able to find a job, about being too old for everything.

'I need and love you more than ever,' he told her.

After two hours of listening to Joe talk, Diane turned round, tears in her eyes, and squeezed his hand.

Then Tom started to cry. Joe and Diane waited expectantly for Wiara to appear but she didn't. So Diane picked up the baby and fed him and burped him and settled him.

Tom, satisfied, cooed contentedly in his cot.

* * *

Wiara left quietly by the back door. They had renewed their faith and didn't need her anymore. But she was also leaving for the sake of her own heart, for she had fallen in love with this little family: daddy and baby and her.

Chapter 31

Tuesday 24th January

Margaret woke up to crisp morning sunshine and an almost overwhelming feeling of nervousness and excitement. Today she was a bride. In four hours' time, she would marry her true love, Walter.

Over the past few weeks, as she prepared for her wedding day, she had decided that a smart suit would be more appropriate for a woman her age than a white dress. Now she stood in front of the mirror wearing her new navy suit, turning this way and that, admiring herself. She certainly looked presentable.

But something had been niggling away at the back of her mind all this time. She'd worn a suit to her first wedding and look how that had turned out. She wanted to do it properly this time. So she'd bought herself a proper wedding dress too, just in case she found she had the courage on the day. She went to the wardrobe and took out the dress. Just then, there was a scratch at her bedroom door, followed by a polite knock.

She opened the door a crack and peeped out to see Walter and Ted standing there.

'Oh, Walter,' she said. 'It's supposed to be bad luck for the groom to see the bride before the ceremony!'

'I know, but I couldn't wait!' Walter said grinning.

'Can I tell you a secret?' Margaret whispered.

Walter put his ear closer to the door.

'I met a gypsy once, and she told me that I'd marry later in life and that it would be the happiest time of my life,' Margaret said. 'I couldn't understand it. I was already married to Mr Brooks then – or thought I was – and I certainly wasn't old … and I was absolutely miserable. I thought she was talking the biggest load of old rubbish. But of course it all makes sense now!'

'I'm not a big fan of this fortune telling malarkey, but maybe she was right. I'll make you happy every single day, even if it kills me.'

'Don't say that.' Margaret slipped her hand out through the open door to hold his. 'You don't know what else she said. She told me that the marriage would be a short one, at the end stage of my life.'

'Oh Margaret, what will be, will be. We're in God's hands. If I die tomorrow I'll be at peace. I woke up this morning and that quiet sadness I've always had was gone! As far as I'm concerned, every day is a bonus. The happiness you've brought me would fill a dozen lifetimes!'

Ted yawned, making Margaret and Walter giggle.

'I'll see you later, my dear,' said Walter, patting Margaret on the hand.

She closed the door and sat down on the bed to compose herself. How had she got so lucky?! She made her decision. Off came the suit and on went the dress. It was a bit of a struggle on her own, but she did it. She hardly dared to look in the mirror. When she did, she couldn't believe her eyes! She never knew she could look so, so … feminine!

* * *

Walter waited at the altar, and as Margaret approached he turned around and said one word: 'Beautiful!'

She was wearing a traditional white dress, and Helen, beaming from ear to ear, was following her down the aisle holding the train.

Joe too was barely recognisable in this suit, his hair slicked back, standing beside Walter; he was best man. Joe kept looking round at the congregation where his wife and baby were sitting, proudly watching the proceedings.

Ted waited for them on the church steps, wearing his new leather collar. Walter had insisted that Ted be there. He was as much a part of their lives as the people there. It was Ted who had led him to Margaret.

Yet Walter knew that there were a few other people Margaret would have liked to be there. So he had invited Rebecca and the children. They arrived late – after the bride – and so they sat down at the back of the church. But Margaret, delighted to see them, walked back up the aisle, trying not to trip on her dress, and led Rebecca and the twins up to the front pew. Rebecca had tears in her eyes. Margaret hugged her and went back to stand beside Walter.

If Margaret had surprised Walter by wearing a proper wedding dress, he had a surprise for her too. He'd always thought he would use his mother's wedding ring if he ever got married, but now that that moment had arrived, he'd decided to buy two new ones especially for him and Margaret. Both rings bore an inscription which he'd also had made into a plaque for their bench: 'If you sit beside me today, I will sit beside you forever.'

As the rings were exchanged so were the vows.

'I do!' he said.

'I do!' she said.

'I pronounce you man and wife!' the minister said.

When Walter kissed Margaret his mind went blank. The only thing that mattered was that kiss in that moment.

* * *

Helen's café was the venue for the reception. It was decorated with brightly coloured balloons and streamers, and 'Congratulations!' banners hung from every wall. It smelled clean and fresh; Helen had worked hard and done them proud. All the tablecloths had been washed, and she had found matching crockery and cutlery for the occasion. Rebecca looked on approvingly and the twins were on their best behaviour. Even the long-awaited sun appeared, pouring through the sparkling clean windows.

Once everyone had had a bite to eat, there was a tinkling of teacups and Joe stood up. Clearing his throat he began, 'I'm not a man of many words ...'

'No, but you're a man of many fry-ups ... and cups of tea,' shouted Helen, laughing. Joe's wife laughed, while baby Tom gurgled happily in her arms. Margaret and Walter smiled as they held on to each other tightly.

'Today is not about me,' Joe went on. 'It's about the faith and hope that Margaret and Walter have inspired in us all over the past few months. I have faith again in God and people and my family. You're never too old to hope.' Wiping his eyes he sat down at the table with the rest of his family while everyone cheered and clapped.

Unexpectedly Rebecca stood up. The room hushed.

'I have known Margaret my whole life. She has been like a mother to me – that's because she truly was my mother. Mum, place your hand on the table.'

Margaret looked puzzled but did as Rebecca asked.

'Walter, place your hand on top of Margaret's,' Rebecca asked. Walter put his hand on top of his wife's.

'Walter, that's the last time you'll get the upper hand on a woman as strong as my mother,' Rebecca said.

Everyone laughed.

She took a deep breath. 'My mother is a strong and loving person,' Rebecca went on. 'And I want to thank her for … *everything*.'

Epilogue

Margaret had a dream that they were sitting on their bench together. She could feel – almost hear – the plants around them growing. They were wearing their honeymoon clothes, bright and cheerful, a challenge to the wet spring weather. But it felt as if they'd been married for years. Margaret watched the scene as if she was an angel floating in the sky.

Ted woofed.

'Settle down boy,' Walter said to the dog.

Ted pulled on his lead, wanting to go for a walk. Walter brought him back. 'What's wrong with you today, Ted?'

Somewhere a firework went off like a starter gun. Ted slipped his lead and darted off, and on and on towards the main road.

'Come back, Ted,' Walter called.

But it was too late; Ted got hit by a car. When Walter caught up with him, he fell to his knees clutching his arm. Ted lay in the gutter not moving.

'No! Not my Ted!' Walter gasped. 'Margaret,' he whispered.

Margaret yelled for help, but could only stand and watch as Walter shuddered and took one final breath. Just as she was kneeling in prayer at his side, she woke up.

She turned to Walter. There he was, sleeping soundly beside her in their warm cosy bed. But something compelled her to touch his forehead. It was cold. He had gone. She put her head on his chest and closed her eyes. She knew that Walter would never leave her and little Ted behind. She drifted off to sleep and had another dream.

In this dream the sun was shining brightly, the leaves were on the trees and the grass was green. Margaret walked slowly to Helen's café, weighed down by life. But through the window, she saw Walter and Ted. In that instant she knew she had nothing to fear. She was home. Margaret went in and sat beside Walter and Ted.

* * *

Margaret, Walter and Ted passed away one Sunday in April. The doctors, after ruling out a gas leak, were unable to find a cause of death. It remains a mystery to this day.

Joe and Diane went on to have two more children, whom they called Margaret and Walter in their memory of their old friends.

The End.

ABOUT THE AUTHOR

This book was written by John Morgan based on a concept by Maria
  Stewart. John is an eternal student of life and lives in Northern
  Ireland.

Printed in Great Britain
by Amazon

73394258R00119